Metaphorosis

March 2019

Beautifully made speculative fiction

Also from Metaphorosis Books

Reading 5X5: Readers' Edition
Reading 5X5: Writers' Edition

Best Vegan Science Fiction & Fantasy

Best Vegan SFF of 2017
Best Vegan SFF of 2016

Metaphorosis Magazine

Metaphorosis: Best of 2017
Metaphorosis: Best of 2016
Metaphorosis 2017: The Complete stories
Metaphorosis 2016: Nearly Complete Stories
Monthly issues

by B. Morris Allen

Susurrus
Allenthology: Volume I
Tocsin: and other stories
Start with Stones: collected stories
Metaphorosis: a collection of stories

Metaphorosis

March 2019

edited by
B. Morris Allen

Metaphorosis Books

Neskowin

ISSN: 2573-136X (online)
ISBN: 978-1-64076-135-3 (e-book)
ISBN: 978-1-64076-136-0 (paperback)

March 2019

Pleasing the Giants............................7
by Carolyn Lenz

Absurd of a Feather............................25
by Amman Sabet

The Noise Inside................................57
by Vaya Pseftaki

L'Appel du Vide................................99
by Rajiv Moté

The Color of My Home is Red Like an Apple
....121
by Evan Marcroft

Pleasing the Giants

Carolyn Lenz

Deiderick raced down the cobblestone street, the hollow sound of his footsteps barely audible over the singing around him. It wouldn't take long for his mother and father to notice him missing. He was supposed to be arranging tulips now, in full view of the giants, just as their boat passed. But they wouldn't ask where he was. They wouldn't show any anger or disappointment in him. Their smiles wouldn't falter, not when the giants might see.

Ducking around a corner to leap a narrow waterway, Deiderick kept his own smile plastered on his face. The people lining the street were singing the same song his parents did, the same song everyone did, but their clothes were different. Similar enough that the giants might not notice that Deiderick didn't belong. The stripes on all the boys' shirts were horizontal, not vertical like Deiderick's, and they wore canal hats instead of berets. The only part Deiderick was worried about was his distinctive wooden shoes.

But he had to go this way.

Just ahead, he spotted his goal. Another boy, singing along with everyone else, smiling along with everyone else, but his arms weren't making the sweeping gestures most of the people were. They were otherwise occupied, working the long pole that powered his gondola. Pushing him toward Deiderick.

Deiderick leapt from the edge of the pier. As he flew towards the small boat, much smaller than the ones the giants used, the gondolier looked up. Spotted Deiderick. The gondolier's eyes went wide – even wider than they normally were, which was exactly as wide as Deiderick's normally were – and he gave a slight shake of his head even as he kept singing.

It was too late. Deiderick couldn't stop if he wanted to.

Not that there was any way he was stopping now. He'd spent years planning this, watching the boats, counting the seconds between them, wandering as far as he could from his family's gardens in the time he wasn't being watched, climbing buildings to get a view of the surrounding area. Learning everything he could during the gaps between the boats. Finally he had understood enough of how his world fit together in order to slip between the cracks, and hopefully come out into the giants' world.

He landed on the deck of the gondola, the force of his jump propelling them out into the wide river, leaving the pier far out of reach. The gondolier tried to steer them back on course, but Deiderick grabbed onto the pole, wrestling it from the gondolier's hands. Not a difficult task. Deiderick knew that what he was doing might displease the giants. So did the gondolier. But it would displease the giants more to fight in front of them, for anyone to act less than completely content. Everyone in Deiderick's village had known that for as long as they could remember. If he got caught, Deiderick could be the first to test that knowledge.

Deiderick kept singing as he steered the gondola on a new course, heading to a neighbouring village. Even though the song was about friendship between everyone, he had never been to any of the other villages. Not until today.

Next to him on the boat, the gondolier sang as well, his eyes glued to Deiderick. And then he looked up. He almost stopped smiling.

Deiderick turned to see what had terrified the gondolier so much. One of the boats, not the gondolas, but the enormous crafts the giants used, was looming over them. Deiderick hadn't even noticed it. The giants' boats glided through the water, not creating any waves or eddies, just seeming to skate along the surface.

The shadow of the massive boat fell over the gondola. The giants disappeared beyond the edge of the railing, only for one to pop out again. There was a bright flash of light as Deiderick stabbed the gondola pole into the bottom of the wide river, plunging it into the rock hard river bed over and over. The gondola barely moved in response.

The giants' boat got closer, only inches away. Dozens of giants were leaning over the side now, peering at Deiderick and the gondolier. The giants had always stayed in their boats, never even reaching out towards any of the villages or villagers, so this was the closest Deiderick had ever been to any of them. They were even bigger than he'd thought, their faces as tall as Deiderick's entire body.

Even staring up at them now, Deiderick had no idea what they wanted from him. He had hoped to find out, but now it didn't look like he was going to learn anything.

In desperation, Deiderick pulled the gondola pole out of the water and jammed it into the side of the giants' boat. With one shove, the gondola slid away, zooming to the other side of the river.

Deiderick held the gondola pole out to the gondolier as he jumped and grabbed hold of one of the rigid green leaves of the next village's overgrown vegetation, climbing onto the shore. The gondolier snatched the pole, his feelings obvious even as he smiled with apparent delight.

Deiderick stopped, dazzled. Everyone in his village wore the same colours, red, white, and blue. The people here wore long robes and dresses, in a rainbow of colours. One of them, a girl with long black hair, smiled at Deiderick, her eyes narrowing a fraction of an inch in confusion. The expression reminded Deiderick to keep moving. He was almost there. He was almost where he'd seen the giant come out of the ground.

He ducked behind a tree and waited until the nearby boat rounded a bend, and then began counting down the seconds. He dropped to his knees and crawled through an archway, feeling the time slipping away from him. Winding his way between minarets, Deiderick started to worry that he'd misjudged the distance. Each second felt like it was a little too fast, each tower too big to get past before the next boat would come.

And then he was there. He was finally somewhere where the giants couldn't see him, at least, not from the boats. He was behind a wall, and he didn't have to smile or sing for anyone. But most of all, he was behind the wall that he'd seen one giant's shoulders hulk up over, crawling through the ground into Deiderick's world. Maybe from here, he'd be able to figure out who the giants were, why they wanted

Diederick and all the other villagers to sing for them.

"Giant?" Deiderick whispered. His voice was masked by the singing in the village behind him, but he didn't know how it would echo behind the wall. He also didn't know how it would sound, on its own, without the chorus. "Hello?" he called, a little louder.

When no one answered after a minute, he crept forward. His wooden clogs tapped against the ground, no matter how softly he tip-toed. He was so careful not to lift them and risk the sound that they almost shuffled across the ground. Until the right clog clanged against something solid.

Deiderick jumped and looked around. The song still ringing in his ears hadn't wavered. No giants were looking over the wall to investigate. No one had noticed. With a sigh of relief, he looked down, wondering what he had kicked.

A large square in the ground was raised a few inches higher than the rest. On one side were large hinges. Giant-sized hinges. With wide eyes – even wider than usual – Deiderick crouched down, staring at the hatch.

His small fingers easily found a gap between the hatch and the ground. He worked them in deeper, getting a grip. Deiderick didn't know if it was because he was so close to answers, or if it was just what he was used to, but a smile grew across his face as he began to lift the hatch.

It came up with little effort – it was heavy, but not as heavy as he expected. Deiderick managed to lift it wide enough to slip under, but the door slammed shut on Deiderick's fingers where he clutched the edge of the opening. With a scream, he found himself falling into the darkness.

His voice cut off with a thud as he hit the ground a second later. Deiderick panted in shock, staring up at the hatch above him. It didn't make sense. The tunnel he was in wasn't big enough for giants, unless they were crawling. Were there others of Deiderick's size, living among the giants?

He stood and listened, worried someone had heard him scream, heard him fall. From here, he could still hear the sound of all the villages singing their same song, but it was echoed and distorted by the long tunnel ahead. Deiderick's smile had long since faded, and now he shivered. The song the giants forced everyone to sing sounded wrong from where he stood. He jumped, flailing for the door above him, but it was out of reach. The tunnel behind him ended abruptly with a huge, unmoving fan. The only way to go was forwards.

At first, Deiderick thought the song echoing behind him was fading, but it soon started getting louder again. It wasn't long before it sounded very close. Deiderick crept forward, worried that the hallway had looped around to deposit him in his village, back where he'd started.

But something about this singing sounded wrong. It was a little too tinny, a little too homogenous. Like many people singing with the same voice.

Light filtered through a large grate embedded in the wall ahead of him. Deiderick peered through one of the slits. He didn't see anything behind it, just blank greyness. He decided to take a chance – he'd come this far. He laced his fingers through some of the openings in the grate and shoved, holding it as still as he could as it popped off. After a moment of waiting to see if anyone had noticed, Deiderick slipped out of the tunnel and propped the grate up behind him.

Outside, the song was much louder, but it obviously wasn't being sung by the people from Deiderick's village, or any of the other villages nearby. Below the sound, there was a low hum, like many people speaking softly. Deiderick was in a narrow passage between the grate he had just exited, and a flat grey wall. Either side of the passage opened up into wide spaces, but all Deiderick could see from where he stood was light and colour streaming in. Deiderick sidled towards the light, leaning out as little as he could to take a peek.

His village stretched out in front of him. Sloping down from the wall he hid behind – the back wall of a large Tudor house – was a town square like the one he'd snuck away from, dotted with people dressed just like his friends and family. Their arms waved in jerky patterns. A hillside dropped away in front of them, but not into water like in Deiderick's village. Here, giants shuffled slowly through the dry riverbed, instead of riding in their silent boats. Some of them watched the tiny villagers, but unlike the giants in the boats, most of them didn't seem interested, talking and laughing amongst themselves.

Hoping the giants weren't paying enough attention to notice him, Deiderick darted out into the open to see who these other villagers were. He raced past a few of the singing people, taking quick glances before ducking behind a nearby house to catch his breath and make sense of what he'd seen.

He felt like his smile had been permanently wiped from his face. The villagers hadn't been singing. How could they be? Their faces were fixed, their mouths permanently stretched open, their eyes glassy and wide. They were fake, some kind of mannequin or dummy, made to look like they were singing and dancing. Deiderick didn't have any idea who the giants were or what they wanted. He had thought that anything he learned could only help him to understand more about the giants, that any explanation would make more sense than none whatsoever. But what he was seeing – he suddenly felt like he knew less than when he'd started.

"Enjoy your ride!" Deiderick heard a bright voice say. He poked his head back around the building, scanning the crowds that wound through the villages, eventually coming to the front of the line, where a cluster of giants was climbing into a boat. A smiling giant closed a gate behind them as she wished them a pleasant trip. A few other giants in line pointed and smiled at something above Deiderick's head. He turned to see a plaque embedded in the wall above him:

These models are the originals that first debuted in 1964 at the New York World's Fair.

"Hey!" Deiderick almost jumped high enough to pop out above the house he hid behind. The furtive whisper had come from over his shoulder. Or, at least, it sounded like a whisper, even though it had the volume of one of Deiderick's shouts.

Deiderick turned, slowly, not wanting to see the giant that he knew was behind him. A giant, his head poking up from underneath the landscape, hidden from view of the long lineup. Deiderick wanted to run, but there was nowhere to go.

"What are you doing here?" the giant asked. He didn't sound angry, like Deiderick had expected. He sounded confused, worried, and – maybe – a little impressed.

Deiderick almost opened his mouth to speak, and then clamped his hand over his mouth. He looked to either side, searching for an exit. There was nowhere to run. Everything around him was too open.

"Hey, I'm not gonna hurt you," the giant said, still whispering.

Why was he hiding from the other giants? Deiderick wondered. Maybe he wasn't quite one of them. Maybe he would help Deiderick.

"I – I just wanted to see," Deiderick said, and then clamped his hand over his mouth again. No one in his village had ever spoken to a giant. It was not allowed. It displeased them. "I'm sorry I'm not singing," he blurted out.

"Why would you be sorry about that?" the giant asked.

"Because it displeases you. Singing is supposed to please the giants."

The giant frowned. Deiderick froze in terror. He didn't know what was supposed to happen when you displeased the giants. No one did. "You aren't..." the giant started, pausing when Deiderick flinched. "Oh god. Can you guys *think*?"

"Y-yes?" Deiderick stammered.

"And you... have feelings? Personalities?"

"Yes," Deiderick said slowly, confused. Couldn't the giant tell? Was Deiderick displeasing him more? "That's how we were made. To please the giants."

"Oh. Oh no," the giant looked horrified. "Did we make you sentient?"

"Not if that displeases you!" Deiderick cried. "I just want to go home."

"Hey. Hey, buddy, don't be scared." The giant's tone was soft, soothing. He wriggled around, manoeuvering his hand up into the hole in the landscape his head occupied. His outstretched palm looked surprisingly inviting to Deiderick. "Come on. I'll take you home."

Another look around confirmed for Deiderick that he had no other option, besides running out from behind the house into the view of hundreds of giants. His head hung low, he stepped onto the giant's hand. In a brisk movement, he was below the copy of his village, dropping in jerks down a ladder that led to a hallway built for giants.

"Where is this place?" Deiderick asked, his voice hushed. His gaze whipped to the giant's face, checking to see if it was displeased that he had spoken.

"This is an access tunnel, for ride maintenance," the giant said.

Speaking hadn't seemed to offend the giant. Deiderick felt brave enough to ask another question. "What do you mean, 'ride'?" he asked.

This actually did make the giant react. His mouth dropped, his eyes went wide, he stared at Deiderick for a moment. "It's, uh, hard to explain."

"What is?"

"Look," the giant sighed, "A ride is a thing you sit on that moves. For fun."

Deiderick decided he was never going to get another chance to ask what he really wanted to know. "Why do the giants always watch us? Why do we have to sing?"

"Because that's the ride. The boats that we, uh, the giants take, those are the ride."

"And it goes through my village?"

"Your village is part of the ride. It is the ride."

"But... Why?"

"For fun."

"Am I on the ride?"

"No, it's —" The giant took a deep breath, trying to think. "People want to see you and your... your village. They want to see you being happy."

"And that's why we sing?"

"Yes!" the giant beamed. "Yes, exactly! We want you to be happy, and sing. That's all we want."

"So, that's it?" Diederick asked with a frown. "That's what the giants want?"

"Yeah," the giant nodded. "That's all it is."

Deiderick silently rode on the giant's shoulder, thinking about what the giant had said. He didn't ask any more questions, even when the giant climbed halfway through something called an access hatch and set Deiderick on the ground behind a building near his village. He kept thinking, all the way through the neighbouring villages, waiting for gaps between the giants' boats. As he made his way back, he started to sing the song he'd been singing, along with everyone else, for as long as he could remember.

Deiderick slipped back into position at his family's bakery to take a tray of bread from the oven. His family's smiles didn't betray their questions about where he had been. He wasn't worried about that. He had bigger things to think about.

The giant had told him to be happy, but why? He had said this was all a ride, but what did that mean? None of what he'd seen, or what the giant had told him, made any sense. It had to be a lie, meant to keep Deiderick from investigating more, asking more questions. He would go back to watching the boats, counting the seconds between them, and learning everything he could during the gaps.

For now, all Deiderick could do was smile and sing. But at least he knew there really was more to life than his small world, after all.

See Carolyn Lenz's story "Pleasing the Giants" online at Metaphorosis.
If you liked it, leave a comment. Authors love that!
Remember to subscribe to our e-mail updates so you'll know when new stories are posted.

About the story

The initial idea for "Pleasing the Giants" came about when I heard a story about a man who successfully sued Disney World for psychological distress when he was trapped on the It's a Small World ride for 40 minutes. Obviously my first thought was to wonder how long I could listen to that song on repeat without having a breakdown, but that led me to think about the employees running that ride, and, finally, what it would be like to be one of the animatronics, if they had inner lives. From that, the structure and feel of the first draft came to me almost fully formed.

A question for the author

Q: Do you use music for inspiration? If so what do you listen to?

A: I use music in two ways when I write. The most basic is less inspiration and more motivation. I'll often listen to video game music during the actual act of writing, since lyrics distract me and video game music is designed to get you in a groove and keep you moving.

The other way I use music is to help clarify characters. If I'm having trouble expressing a character's perspective or motivation, I'll try to think of what their personal theme song would be. I find you can have a very clear image of who a character is in your head without necessarily having the words to describe it, and music and the feelings evoked by it can really help to bridge that gap.

About the author

Carolyn Lenz is a scientist, writer, and badass from Hamilton, Ontario. She has written speculative fiction for eight years, mostly for fun and sometimes for profit, using her knowledge of science and unique way of looking at the world to create strange characters and places. By day, she wears a lab coat and works with unsettling amounts of human blood.

@SeaLenz

Absurd of a Feather

Amman Sabet

I'm getting a note from my doctor that will keep me out of the pool for gym. It's not that I can't swim. Last year I came in third place for breast stroke. This is different. I'm uncomfortable with taking my shirt off now, and I'd rather spend the period studying in the library while the other kids do laps and cannonball into the deep end.

"Terrence," my doctor tells me in his examining room. "It's a confusing time for boys your age. Your hormones make you crazy and you go through these changes. It's nothing to—"

That's when he sees what's been bothering me. An anomalous little hole has opened in the center of my chest. It looks like a puckered divot, like my belly button, but smaller and over my sternum.

He hums and presses his fingers around my ribs. "Does that hurt? Did you injure yourself somehow?"

I say no.

"Have you put anything into it, like the tip of a pencil?"

Nope.

"Well, let's keep an eye on it. Make sure the area stays dry and clean and I'm going to give your mom the number to a specialist at the VA who deals with these kinds of things. Listen, kiddo, you're not the only senior with pectoral developments like this. We've been seeing this sort of thing pretty commonly with the active-duty families out here. Usually just a benign cosmetic mutation, like webbed toes. We'll sort it out."

Doc ends our visit on a casual note, but when I get home that evening I can't help myself from searching for deformities online again. Cobbler's chest. Extra nipples. There is nothing like my hole and the more I search, the more hideous and deformed I feel.

In front of the bathroom mirror, I swab the area around the hole with rubbing alcohol. Then, gingerly, I spin a Q-tip around inside the opening. It seems shallow, but I still have a premonition that I might somehow poke my internal organs and the thought makes me dizzy and sick. I put a band-aid over it.

I live just outside of Petaluma, where the farmland blends with the suburban sprawl and it smells faintly like cow poop everywhere. Mom's a dental assistant in town. Dad's a chief on a Coast Guard frigate, so he splits his time between the boat and home. When he's not out at sea we toss the ball around and build things in the backyard after I do my homework. Mom and Dad and I spend weekends together and sometimes go on road trips. Mom says she likes it better this way because they argue less.

Walking to the bus stop for school, I hear a crystalline jingle over the wind and notice that someone has finally rented that old shingled house at the end of our road. The new neighbors have hung wind chimes over the front porch. A man is unloading moving boxes from a moving trailer. Hoisting one up the stairs towards the front door, he reaches up and swats the wind chimes with his hand, making the sound again.

A family wagon—looking like it has been on a long and muddy drive—backs out of the garage. I don't want the new neighbors to think I'm being nosy, so I duck behind a tree on the sidewalk and pretend to cuff my jeans. I don't know why it doesn't occur to me to just say hello and introduce myself. I catch Minnesota plates as they pass.

There's a girl in the back seat who's maybe a year older than me. She's wearing an olive-green parka. Too warm for California. It's only momentary, but I notice her blonde hair and pretty, angular profile. I wonder if her parents are dropping her off at school and if I'll see her there.

I put my bag in my locker and keep an eye out for the girl and her parka. She isn't at first period English or at second period Geometry. There's no sign of her in the lunch room or any of the common areas either. It dawns on me that wherever she is, she probably took her coat off, anyway. Maybe she enrolled at the Catholic school?

By the time gym class swings around, I've forgotten all about her. While my classmates swim, I sit in the library at the long study table in the main area, scratching band logos on my binder with a ballpoint and absently rubbing the band-aid under my shirt with my thumb. The clock is the loudest thing in the library.

It's not until the end of the period that I look up and spot the new girl hunched over in her big green parka behind the backrest of one of the swiveling reading chairs. Her backpack is propped up between her sneakers and she is completely still.

The bell rings. I put my books back in my bag and make for the door, but she still hasn't moved. Her hood covers her face.

"Hey," I say, wanting to wake her so she won't miss her next period. She doesn't move. "Hello?"

When I touch her shoulder, she wakes with a shudder. Her parka hunched up like that gives the impression she probably doesn't like to be interrupted (who does, really?). But she doesn't look pissed. If anything, she looks embarrassed, and wipes her mouth where she drooled a little.

"Sorry," I mumble. "It's next period."

Glancing up at the clock, she grabs her backpack and then rushes out ahead of me. Out in the hallway, she has vanished among the flocks rushing to next period.

At night, I undress for bed. With my shirt off, I notice on my chest, near the band-aid covering the hole, a bit of lint from my shirt. I try to brush it off. But it sticks. Upon closer inspection in the mirror, it's actually fuzz. Not lint. Not hair. Not fur. Fuzz.

Under the band-aid, the hole is still there. I don't know why I thought it would have closed. Fretting, I pinch some of the fuzz around the hole and try to pull it out, but it hurts. I yank some out anyway, with a little yelp. Red dapples of blood rise up from the skin. It's too painful, so I stop and yell downstairs to my mom that I want to see the doctor again.

The new girl is there in the library again. She emerges from the history stacks and sits at the table by the *Indian Nations* poster, leafing through a book with white doves on the cover. It's just the two of us there. I figure I should say something so it's not weird.

"*Hooow*," I bellow, saluting her as I imagine a Sioux brave would greet a tribe member. Awkward.

She looks around the room, unsure if I'm talking to her. "Did you just say something?"

"Uh, sorry. I'm Terry. You moved in down the street from me? The house with the shingles?"

"Oh, hey. Terry. Yeah, that's us with the trailer." She says my name right away as if committing it to memory, like I could have a part to play in the cast of people she sees every day at school. She holds out her hand. "Ontario."

"Cool name."

"Thanks. It's where my folks met."

She tells me that she has a doctor's note and I laugh, explaining that I have one too. We compare different teachers at school, the other classes she's taking. As I describe our neighbors, she closes her book to listen. Gradually, I steer towards asking about her friends, what it's like where she's from. Maybe gauge if there's a boyfriend in the picture.

"We're a Coastie family too," she says. "Mom started doing web design after her commission. Dad's a warrant officer. We transitioned from Michigan to the base out in Point Reyes 'cause the schools are better."

"So... a bunch of us are going to Red Bridge this weekend," I offer. "It's just this place where the kids from the neighborhood hang out. Wanna come with?"

Ontario nods eagerly. She seemed timid when I first met her, but she doesn't hide wanting to have friends like kids our age learn to do. I'm a little concerned that my friends might prey on that kind of vulnerability, the way she chooses not to mask herself despite being a new face. Then again, I kind of hope they'll be disarmed by her forthright friendliness like I am. It's like she's never had a person in the world be cruel to her, or has risen above it somehow. *God, why am I thinking like this?*

I've been sitting very upright in my seat and smiling for so long that my cheeks are sore now. My chest is tight, sort of an ache. When I press my thumb against my shirt I can feel the divot, the fabric sliding against the edges.

"Everything okay?" Ontario asks.

"Huh?"

"You made a weird face."

"Oh, I'm good," I say. "Just, uh, dying for study hall to be over, right?"

Later, after school, I find a couple of twenties under the key dish at home with a note: *Conference until Mon. This is for pizza. Don't forget your doctor's appointment in case I don't see you. Hugs, Mom.*

I'm so glad to have broken the ice with Ontario that I've forgotten all about my problem. In the upstairs bathroom, I take my shirt off to clean the hole in my chest and I'm startled to discover that what was fuzz before has spread out more from the center. The patches closer to the hole have grown rigid, like the vanes of tiny feathers.

Horrified, I pull my shirt down. I don't even want to look at what's going on with my chest anymore. The doc can just burn it all off next week with acid or whatever he's got in those cabinets in his office.

Red Bridge is a small span of elevated road gliding over an inlet to the marshlands. There aren't too many houses out there, so it's secluded. At night, kids park their cars and lock their bikes at the end of the bridge and walk out to the middle and climb over the guardrail. The piers stick out from the side facing the sound, enough that there's a ledge where we can sit and drink beers and dare each other to jump. It's not that far of a drop, but the water is gross and there are a few rusty shopping carts that stick out from the surface at low tide.

In the dark, I can hear my friends' hysterics echoing over the marshlands and the thrum of the crickets. The moon is a sliver-smile winking over the inlet.

"Terry?" Ontario startles me, her voice is so close. "I thought that was you."

"Phew," I say. "It's freaking dark. You almost gave me a heart attack."

There's a heavy, clinking plastic bag by her feet. I wonder at first why she hasn't crossed yet, but then I remember she doesn't know anyone and was waiting for me with this armload of wine bottles.

We walk across the bridge together. She holds the bag as if the bottom might fall out and explains how she snagged the wine from her dad's moving boxes. She says they won't be missed, but I can tell her dad will be mad when he finds out and she just doesn't care about that right now.

At the middle of the bridge, we step over the guard rail and climb down to the pylon where everyone is sitting. I introduce Ontario and people ask whose classes she's in. They're all super glad that she brought some wine with her because the others with ID haven't shown up.

It's windy, huddled against each other. We can't figure out how to open the wine because Ontario didn't bring a corkscrew, but someone succeeds in pushing the cork into one of the bottles after chiseling at it with an old nail. We play music on one of our phones, barely audible over the wind as we pass the bottle. It tastes really bitter.

The guys in the group are either drunk or acting like it. They tease her because of her name, saying things like "beg my pard, I'm out for a rip" and "got my gonch in a bunch, hey?" in this horrible fake Canadian accent.

She laughs, more at them because they all have purple wine-stained teeth. One of them throws an empty bottle up in the air and it smashes on the asphalt in the middle of the bridge, so much louder than anything else. Everyone ducks low. We keep quiet, looking for lights in windows, listening for the neighbors who might've heard the shatter.

With our hoods up, Ontario and I creep over to the pylons on the other side of the bridge, out of the wind, where things aren't falling and no one can see us. Sneakers dangling, she shares a cigarette she has rolled and talks about how I remind her of someone at her old school that she used to go out with.

My pocket lights up with a text asking where we went. Some of the others are planning on watching a movie and smoking weed in someone's garage. I turn to Ontario and ask her what she wants to do and she shrugs. There's an awkward silence and I don't know if she wants to go hang out with them, or if she wants to go home, or if she wants to stay back with me at the bridge. Neither of us say anything when we hear the others asking where we went. Neither of us say anything when we hear their car doors opening and the faint ping of the seatbelt alert through their muted laugh-talking in the distant dark.

"Are you going to kiss me?" she asks.

"Okay."

I lean in halfway and she's so tense looking, like she's bracing herself. She turns and our mouths bump together gently, like we were both about to whisper something and instead had a little pillowy fender bender. Her lips are thin and I can feel how their edges curl against mine. The tip of her nose is cold.

Our hands and arms are an entangled scaffolding of sorts, crumpling at the elbows as we pull close. My hand, first at her hip, follows up the warm curve of her waist, up and under and—*goose down? What kind of bra is she wearing?*

"Whoah, wait, no."

"Oh. Sorry."

Breaking liplock, I disentangle my hand from her sweatshirt, and I'm not sure if what I'm seeing is right. Soft white down covers the front of her chest. It extends from the top of her abdomen to just below her collarbone. A few longer wispy feathers radiate from the center like a star.

"It's just my undershirt," she blurts, pulling her knees to her chest, sweatshirt over knees. A half-breath of stunned silence. Then she uncurls and moves to climb back over the guard rail. "I have to go home."

"Wait! I have to show you something," I offer. "Give me a second, okay? I have to take this off."

Ontario gets that petrified expression on her face again, like I'm putting another move on her, so I put some distance between us. I know if she sees my chest, she'll know I have it too. Maybe she can tell me what it is.

I stretch my arms back and fill my lungs with air. It's a weird sensation. Arching my shoulders makes this spasm roll up my chest cavity. I pull my windbreaker off, then unbutton my shirt halfway before I decide to just yank it over my head along with my undershirt.

My chest is tingling, like when your hair stands up, except it's the feathers. They've grown out more, all vibrating and fanned out over my chest. I know if I look down that I'd see their glossy plumes reaching further from the center where my hole is. I puff my chest out, stick my elbows out at the sides, making myself as broad as possible. I didn't think I'd actually show off. It's weird. I thought it'd be a more modest reveal, but it just feels good to finally be seen. I'm driven to strut, just a little, from side to side like some kind of rooster, stretching my shoulders back. *This is ridiculous.*

Ontario holds her hand to her mouth. Then shuffles off her sweatshirt. Her feathers are frillier than mine and white, waving forwards and backwards, buffeting the air between us like a burlesque fan. She has a hole in the center of her chest too, like mine, just over her sternum.

"See? What is this?" I ask. "I don't understand why—"

"Don't talk right now," she says, and rests one of her hands against my feathers. They crinkle a little under her palm. The dull white light from the moon and the lamps at the end of Red Bridge reflect off her white down. This vulnerability is passing between us—this vibe. I want to hold her against me. Just for a moment of normalcy.

We put our arms around each other's shoulders, waists, slowly, like grade-schoolers wondering how closely they should dance. And, by some strange instinct, we press our feathers together in a susurrous embrace, plumage hidden between our bodies. As if we've trapped a glowing cinder between us, the dry warmth spreads up to where my neck is craning helically around hers.

The nape of her neck is flush and warm against my collarbone and I let out a hum. It begins at first as a sigh, but then she's humming too. We both intone and I feel it in her neck through mine. The resplendent vibes, they tickle something inside our necks like there's another vocal cord there. Maybe if I hum harder I might be able to vibrate it in my own neck. As I do, so does she. The warmth unfurls. Holding back a bit, I croon louder for the chord, find it by her collarbone. This unleashes some latent pocket of twinge, causing her neck to twist against mine. Our necks elongate, twisting upwards towards the moon. The crickets fall silent in the dark.

Mouths open, we sing a piercing arpeggio of avian chirps together that echo over the marsh inlet. Birdsong, emitting from the strange vocal cords by our collarbones, modulated by the warmth between us and the shape of our mouths and tongues. Her notes are higher pitched and crack in falsetto. I give tremolo by vibrating my jaw. We harmonize octaves and the ember sandwiched between us pulses out wave after heady wave.

When the rush has passed, my neck snaps stiffly back into shape and I stagger against the bridge, confused. I can't believe what just happened. *But wait, what did just happen?* I want to be on the same page as her because I think that nothing else in the world could be like us. Even if what we did was wrong, in some ways it was right and those are the only ways that matter now.

"We shouldn't have done that," she says, straightening her clothes.

I try to explain how I feel, about how the rightness can only be measured by us. Because it's rare and we are probably the only ones who are like this. My words don't come out that way though. I sound like a babbling idiot and the expression on her face tells me I'm only making matters worse.

"Really, I need to go home." Pushing past me, she grabs her parka and climbs back over.

"Can't we just talk about this? Ontario..." Down the bridge, she doesn't respond. In the dark, I hear the rattle of her bike chain as she pedals away.

Sunday morning comes. In the mirror, the feathers are now darker, straighter, overlapping in spots. Pressing my palm against them feels like what I imagine the tail of a duck would feel like. The plumage is light and soft and for some reason it doesn't seem as hideous anymore. I look at them from the front, the side. *Am I going crazy, or is my sternum just slightly pronounced?*

I ping Ontario. *Can we talk?*

I'm snubbed when ten minutes pass and she doesn't hit me back. Then twenty. No response. And, as if a switch has been thrown, once again I feel hideously deformed. I pray the doctor can make my chest normal. Maybe give me experimental hormones or graft skin from somewhere. I'd rather have a scar on my chest than some weird feathered hole. I'm anxious to deal with my problem as soon as possible.

Hoping beyond reason that getting baked with my friends can cram these thoughts back into the recesses of my mind, I text them to swing by in the battlewagon. But when I'm smashed between two of them in their hotboxed back seat, they're loud and obnoxious and won't stop plying me for details over the stoner metal galloping out of the speakers.

"So? What's she like? Did you do it? Did you bump uglies?"

Their questions are cruel and edged, like they want to hack down something that could've been special before they even learn if it was or not, and I wonder if they are really my friends. Bombing around in their shitbox and listening to their nonsense, I've had it after only a few minutes. I'm having a hard time breathing anyway. It's like cottonmouth in my lungs. I tell them to just swing by my house and let me out.

Having seen each other at our most vulnerable, maybe the feathers are a sign, like Ontario and I were supposed to have met. It's like some force field has risen around the idea of her that no fear or paranoia can penetrate. These manic notions of romance roll through in waves and I have to remind myself to get a grip.

I text her again. *Ontario, please. We need to talk.*

And even though I don't want to sound like a creepy stalker guy for whom the unwritten rules of texting decorum fly out the window, not having any answers about what passed between us is driving me cuckoo crazy.

In my room, I open my window. It's beginning to feel like no matter how deeply I breathe, I can't get enough air. Like I didn't chew properly and a piece of food is stuck halfway down to my stomach. I can't focus on homework. Or the internet or TV or anything because my breath is so short and I wonder *is this what a panic attack is?* I'm desperate to feel some cold air on my face and stride out to my back yard.

The tree house I built with dad is still there. It's just a simple platform nailed against the trunk with a few support beams and a ladder. It seemed big and high up in the branches when I was a kid, but now I can reach up and touch it easily with the tips of my fingers. Mold and moss grows in patches along the underside.

At four in the morning on Monday, I wake with a sudden sense of urgency and run to the bathroom. I lift my shirt. The feathers are gathered there like a pile of leaves doused in ink, overlapping to the point where I can no longer see skin.

There's a sore bulge between my pectoral muscles, as if a hard, cystic pocket has lodged itself there, pressing against my sternum below the skin. If I pat the feathers down, I can feel around it with the tips of my fingers. It's symmetrically circular, like a great big angry zit. I test it, pressing my hands together, and something crests through the opening of the hole.

"Ugh!"

The hard, round thing slips back into me, the lip of the hole closing elastically back over it. I feel faint. The bathroom gets dim despite the overhead sconce and I run the faucet cold over my wrists, trying to cool my pulse. *I need to get this thing out of me. Right now.*

With the sink basin filled, I press again and the hole opens around it, yellow like the color of pale bile. If I tap it with my nail, I can feel it's not really connected to me, just sort of lodged in there. Whatever it is, I don't want to break it apart while it's still in me because it might poke my insides.

Thinking this is going to require some strain, I grab a towel and lean over the sink. I feel around it again, flexing my chest for leverage, but as it crests, it slips out as the hole sphincters around the other end of it. *Plop* it goes, into the sink. An egg the size of a small fist. Shivers ripple through my chest cavity, ruffling my feathers.

Mom is going to be back from her conference today. If I don't go to school, she'll receive a call. I can't just leave this egg thing swaddled in the towel on my desk. What if it starts to smell and she finds it? I decide I have to go to class with it in my bag. I don't want to look at it. I want to get rid of it, but at the same time I feel duty-bound to make sure it's safe and that nobody sees it.

Passing the other kids who are late for first period, I hold my arm over my bag to keep it from being crushed. Through the nylon of my backpack, I feel how round it is, a reminder that this egg is alive and needs to be kept warm.

I can't hear anything in US History. Sweat builds underneath my hoodie and I can't keep my eyes off of the round shape it's making against the top of my backpack. Thankfully, the teacher doesn't call me, because I might blurt out the word "egg" as the answer to any question. Then I think what might happen if it hatches inside my bag.

Jesus. What if it did? In the short time since Ontario and I did… did that thing we did, I *laid* this thing. *What if the time it takes to hatch is fast too?* I start to get dizzy. I raise my hand and ask to be excused, barely hearing my own words, but my teacher takes one look at me and suggests that I go see the nurse.

In the last stall in the bathroom, I'm afraid to unzip the bag and look at it, but I do. I regret the decision immediately. It's no longer just a gross sort of yellow. Now the egg is riddled with different-sized polka dots. The colors all clash, as if a tiny clown had snuck into my bag and painted it like a fucked-up Easter egg. *Did it get bigger?* I think about flushing it but it's too wide in circumference and I'd have to crush it with something in the toilet bowl.

Gym period rolls around and I've skipped most of my classes. I'm hiding behind the library shelves, waiting in ambush for Ontario to show up. It's not until the last few minutes of the period when she turns up and returns a book she checked out. She looks around the library. When she doesn't see me, I know she has the same idea as I do, because she ducks into one of the reading rooms and closes the door behind her.

I follow her in.

"Oh great," she says, pulling her parka's hood back.

"Look, I'm not going all psycho," I tell her. "You just have to look at this."

I put my book bag on the table, unzip it and peel the panel back to show her the egg. The white overhead lights make the colors look even weirder than they are. Ontario scowls.

"You have to help me with this," I plead.

"Yeah, right," she says incredulously. "You probably stole an ostrich egg from the science lab or something. Why would you joke? When we have the same condition, the same medical—"

She trails off, and I can see her mind working as she searches my face for hints. First hoping that I'm not making fun of her. Then hoping that I am. She slides down the desk away from my bag to sit in another chair.

"What are we going to do about this? Do we go to the nurse?"

"That's not mine," she blurts.

"Ontario. We made this thing together."

"You can't—that's not my thing. You do whatever you want with it. It's not my problem." She's talking fast, throwing up her words in front of her like obstacles.

I'm about to protest, but there's a rustle. Both of us look down at my bag. After a few seconds, the egg moves again, very gently, as if its center of balance has just tumbled. It wobbles onto its side and rolls down slowly down the desk towards her.

"Ugh!" she yelp-screams, and grabs a book out of her bag and hurls it, glancing it off the side of the egg. The egg spins and rolls off the table, and I wince, awaiting the deep resonant crunch from it splattering on the floor, but no. It fell into one of the chairs! Balanced in the center of the cushion divot. Ontario grabs another textbook out of her bag.

"Stop, no!"

But she hurls this book too, hitting the backrest. The chair teeters and falls onto its back with a springy *thwap* against the carpet. The egg rolls, wobbling along the floor past the other chairs and Ontario shoves me aside, clambering after it, over the study table to the other side.

"You'll break it—"

"Out of the way!"

Yanking her boot off, she has this urgent, unreasoning look in her eye like she's trying to splatter a large bug and nothing else matters. I wonder if this mania is part of the whole absurd thing we did, like some reverse maternal instinct. It's clear she doesn't even care about whatever mess would result from such a berserk clobbering.

I snake myself under the table, just managing to intercept the egg with my fingertips to pull it to my chest as her boot heel clubs the carpet with a hollow thud. I roll back under and away. We circle the table, me trying to get to the door with the egg cradled in my arms, Ontario with her hair in her face, eyes like saucers, boot dangling from her clenched fist. I don't understand why she'd destroy the egg, when it's clear to me it needs to be kept safe.

The moment is interrupted when the librarian saunters in and announces "Okay, you two. That's a warning. I'm going to need to ask the two of you to—"

I break for the door, pushing past the librarian and scampering from the study room. Down the metal stairs, I shoulder-check the crash bars leading out past the hallway lockers. The librarian calls after the two of us, telling us not to run.

Having lost Ontario after speed walking through the guy's locker room next to the gym, I don't know what to do with this egg. The logical, pragmatic part of me thinks that maybe somewhere out in the marsh out by Red Bridge would be the right place to deposit it, but another part of me feels like it's my job to make sure that it stays safe.

When I get home, my mom is mad that she had to reschedule the doctor's appointment that I missed. I tell her I can't talk right that second and run up to my room with my bag. I can't remember how the egg's dots were patterned when I last saw them but I swear they've shifted when I open my bag again. Little wobbly stripes have emerged along the surface, diving in and out between the dots.

It's impossible to think even beyond the next ten minutes with my mom still yelling from the bottom of the stairs up after me. The only sensible thing I can think of to do is to stash it somewhere. Maybe in the basement, beside the hot water tank? Or in my closet? No, if I leave it in the house, she'll find it.

When mom moves off, I gather some old blankets from the linen closet where my old baseball equipment is stored. With the egg in my backpack, I sneak out through the kitchen door, back out to the tree house in the woods past the edge of our back yard. The wooden ladder leading up the trunk is all rotten and unstable, so I stand where the lower slats are nailed into the bark. Reaching up, I arrange the blankets into a swaddle, close to the tree trunk, with the egg in the center cupped under my old catcher's mitt.

I check my phone. Nothing from Ontario. I think about arguing with her that she's responsible because she's the mom, but then I remember that it was me that laid it. I think about how fucked this whole thing is. All my thoughts are bent towards how I can entangle her in sharing her half of the responsibility. I don't want to be the only one to decide. I feel like a freak and I don't want to be alone.

That night, Ontario sends an email from an address that I think she created just to send me a message.

Terry,

Look, I'm really sorry for hooking up with you, but we have to get rid of whatever that thing is. Don't tell anyone where it came from because you'll sound crazy, and I'll deny everything anyway.

Dad took my phone away because of the wine. Don't text me because he'll read it, and he'll probably do something we both don't want. Mom got in touch with a specialist through the VA for my thing. We're going down to the South Bay for the surgery.

Ontario

Trying to read between the lines of her email, something crushes inside me under a flash of anger. Maybe I'm mad at myself for having believed that a silly little paradise could subsist between two kids our age. Or maybe I'm just mad at her for not having any answers, just like me.

In a flight of fury, I run over to her house in the dark. The lights are off and the rooms are quiet and empty. I tap her window with a pebble once, then twice, but there is no response and I notice that the wind chimes aren't hanging from her porch anymore. When I peer into the garage door windows, their car isn't there.

Morning. I wake in my bed to discover that my feathers have all molted and fallen out, leaving my chest bare. I find them inside my pajama shirt and scattered under my sheets. You'd think this would be a welcome relief, but it's not. When I touch my chest, I feel the smooth, ordinary skin, and know that something fantastic has ended.

The hole is still there, but it seems smaller.

Before my doctor's appointment, I sprint out to my tree house to check on my egg. I know I want to do the right thing, I just don't know what that is. I'm running on instinct now. I know I'm just a kid. I can try, even if it's just me. Crossing my back yard, I think what it would be like to be born unloved, unwanted, and my heart breaks a little. Everything deserves a little bit of grace, even if a place can't be made for it. *It will be okay,* I think. *I can do this. I'll care for it. I can...*

When I climb the ladder, there is my baseball mitt, turned over. The shell, cracked open, is leaning on its side. Something small and weak has freed itself and escaped into the night to search for warmth. The little colorful fragments of shell, skittering across the wood platform, look like confetti in the breeze.

See Amman Sabet's story "Absurd of a Feather" online at Metaphorosis.
If you liked it, leave a comment. Authors love that!
Remember to subscribe to our e-mail updates so you'll know when new stories are posted.

About the story

This story was directly inspired by "Black Hole" By Charles Burns and "Uzumaki" by Junji Ito. However, I am sure there were many subconscious elements at play. when I wrote "Absurd of a Feather", I was interested in the beauty and intimacy of what it feels like to find someone who is like you, contrasting that with the fear and shame of being abnormal and how that drives young people away from embracing themselves.

A question for the author

Q: What happens when you hit writer's block head on?

A: I go to museums. I move my body. I try to return to the substantially less interesting story of my own life for a bit rather than linger in front of a blank page. When I'm blocked, it's usually because I've become a "dry sponge". Once I've sopped up a bit of inspiration, I don't write. I draw for a bit. I find that when I draw, I often tell myself the story of what is happening as I put the drawing to the page. That doesn't always unblock me, but it does help.

About the author

Amman Sabet is a design strategist and author living and working in Los Angeles. He is a graduate of Clarion, an autodidact, avid poké connoisseur, and enjoys the discovery in trial and error.

@ammansabet

The Noise Inside

Vaya Pseftaki

Sheyen swallows hard and his ears pop. The Noise stops. *How long did it last this time?* He glances at the water-clock fixed on the wall. Longer than before.

It first came a month ago, on his fourteenth birthday, along with the hair. That day, he woke up to a humming, drenched in sweat and with the smooth skin of his head itching. And no matter how hard he tried, he couldn't pinpoint where the humming was coming from. Until Sediniel barged in and, by the horrified look on her face, he could tell; the Noise came from him. When it stopped, minutes later, hair had grown out of his head, blond and smooth, already an inch long. And since then, every time the Noise came, the hair grew.

Sheyen kicks the sheets off.

Footsteps on the corridor outside. He springs up, grabs the brush Mom gave him and starts brushing his hair.

"Sheyen?" It's Sediniel. "Come on, you're not even half-ready yet!" She stops under the doorframe, peeks over her shoulder and slips inside, carefully closing the door behind her. Her brand-new tattoos sway gently on the hairless skin of her head, long red strands like kraal-weed rocking in the sea current. She tiptoes her way to the armoire and throws his good shirt at him.

"Get dressed or fake sick," she says, arms crossed on her chest. "And stop making the Noise. I could hear it next door. Just for today, please?"

Sheyen's tongue feels rough. He swallows. His ears pop. His eyes linger on her wavering tattoos as she comes and sits beside him. He would have gotten them too, on his birthday, a month ago, if it weren't for the hair that had ruined it all.

"Was it louder this time?" he asks and keeps brushing. But Sediniel has already fished the yellow book from under the beddings. *The In-Betweens: a Folk-Tale.*

"Not this bullshit again!" she says and squeezes the book so hard her knuckles turn white. "You are not an In-Between. In-Betweens do not exist. They are monsters our people invented because they shit their pants whenever they come across anything foreign, anyone that's not Vensymari."

"That's what your dad says?" he snaps. Sediniel and her wisecrack opinions. Would she be so eloquent if it were her with the hair and the Noise? No, she could never be in his place; his half-sister is a full Vensymari — not like him. She is Delyan's legitimate child, all hairless and perfect, and her Art works just fine; no weird Noise emanates from inside her, creeping people out.

"That's the truth," Sediniel says. "And it's *our* dad."

"He's just Delyan for me." He snatches the book from her hands and tucks it under the mattress. "Ready for your big day?" He pulls his hair up in a tight ponytail, hoping it will draw less attention at the lunch party. His hands are sweaty.

Sediniel nods and sits a little closer, so close he can hear her breathing.

"The tattoos look nice," he says. "Do they wiggle in the wind?"

"They'd better, unless they used the wrong ink."

"Don't worry, they're already moving."

Sediniel stretches her neck to catch a glimpse of them on the large mirror across the room.

"The official mark of the Vensymari Artists. You'll outshine them all in the Academy," he says and playfully threatens to touch them with his index.

"Hey! They still hurt." She slaps his hand away.

"Is everyone here already for the lunch party?" he asks and puts his shirt on, fumbling with the buttons.

"Lorna, Berthelen, and Phelien arrived with their parents an hour ago. Haven't seen them yet. The others couldn't make it, a storm is brewing across the channel." Sheyen traces a shadow in her voice. "So that just leaves us, dad, my mom, and our three dear friends with their parents."

He wipes his sweaty palms on his knees. He should try to be happy for her today. His state is not her fault.

"Come on, why the sad face? You've been accepted into the Academy. It's your first day as an Artist, with the tattoos and all. You're a full citizen now!"

"The lunch party is stupid," she says and straightens the sharp crease in her trousers, eyes flying back to the mirror to steal glimpses of the tattoos swaying as she moves.

"It's the custom. It wouldn't look good if Delyan didn't host a lunch party for you. It's embarrassing enough that I wasn't accepted in the Academy," Sheyen says, struggling to keep a level voice. He gropes his pockets for any forgotten candy. He finds none.

"I'd rather we went swimming, just the two of us. I'll get plenty of Lorna and her gang this year in the Academy. And, anyway, they're only here to gossip."

Yes, gossip about his hair and the Noise and how he's probably turning into an In-Between. His eyes fall on the floor. He's not the only one disappointed with the turn of events. Sediniel also thought they would leave the house together, off to new adventures, to be trained in the Art, off to adulthood. She might be one of Delyan's four legitimate children, but her other brothers are much older, already scattered around the country, always away. She and Sheyen were born only a month apart, and the scandal of a bastard child had swept Vensymar like no other. But Delyan was firm on not sending Sheyen away to the islands, to Caprish, his Mom's homeland. He had kept him close, raised him along with Sediniel. Mom never ceased being Delyan's mistress, just as she never ceased flaunting her Caprishi heritage; her hair always long and braided in complex coifs, her clothes always a shade of blue or white, her accent always heavy. But Delyan was the First Artist, and just like that, the whole thing had been brushed aside as another harmless quirk of his. It helped that Sheyen at least looked Vensymari. Until the hair grew out and reminded everyone who his Mom was.

"Don't worry, we'll just eat quickly and then we'll go swimming. And I promise I won't say anything stupid to your friends," he says and gets up.

"They were your friends too, a month ago."

Sheyen licks his lips; they're slightly chapped.

"Well, now they think I'm an In-Between."

"That's so stupid. In-Betweens are monsters—"

"With twisted Art and a mane," he says, without turning to look at her. "Maybe it's not that stupid. The stories say that In-Betweens are half-Vensymari —"

"And what's the other half, huh? Does the book say that they're half-Caprishi?"

"The stories don't specify what the other half is. It's not important. What matters is that they're not Vensymari," he says through clenched teeth.

"What, do you think that all half-Vensymari children turn out to be In-Betweens? Yes, they might be rare, but don't you think we would know if people of mixed inheritance turned into monsters?"

"Have you ever seen another half-Vensymari? The borders have been strictly regulated for the past fifty years, so how the Salt would we know? And all the signs are here; In-Betweens are supposed to grow hair all over their bodies and their eyes change color. They say weird things happen around them and that Noise is weird, isn't it now?" A knot is climbing up his throat and he speaks louder to push it down. "They say In-Betweens can put a hole through the world and go to this place of theirs, where they belong. It's even said they trick Vemsymaris to follow them and let them rot in there, lost in a strange land that looks like home but isn't."

The knot won't go away no matter how loud he shouts. The lunch party is going to be a disaster. Sediniel puts her arm around his shoulders; her skin feels cold against the light fabric of his summer shirt.

"No matter what they say, I like your hair. It's like your mom's." Sheyen bites his lips. It's sunny, but he shudders. "It's just one day, don't let Lorna and her gang get to you. I'm sure dad will get you into the Academy next year. Your Art is just different. He'll figure something out."

"Delyan hasn't got the slightest clue what's wrong with me. It's been a month and even he, the First Artist, can't explain it. Neither the Noise nor the hair." He accidentally bites the inside of his cheek and lets out a yelp. "At least if he and Mom let me cut it... The Noise might stop then."

"They can't let you do that. It's against the law for a non-Vensymari."

He looks at her. It's unfair. He shouldn't be ruining her party. His tongue tastes like wet cotton.

"Dina, maybe I should stay here. I can't control the Noise. It just comes," he admits, as he did to their father before.

"No," she says and pulls him to his feet.

"I can't even tell what it sounds like for you all. For me, it's like a ringing in my ears. And lately it's getting so loud you could hear it next door." *Of course she did, I bet they heard it all the way down to the kitchen.*

Sediniel pulls his ponytail gently and pats his shoulder.

"Dad will figure it out. Next year we'll be in the Academy together." Sheyen gazes into the mirror, at them standing side by side, her a bit taller than him. "We look fine," Sediniel says and opens the door.

Sediniel was right; he should have played sick instead of joining the party. Sheyen can barely sit still and listen, eat and listen, drink and listen to them all celebrating. Even Latima's delicious food fails to distract him. A sudden headache splits his thoughts in half; his ears start ringing.

"Can you hear it too?"

Sheyen does not look up; he only catches glimpses of the others out of the corner of his eye. *Please, not now.* No one is talking, forks and fish knives frozen midair, steam wafting. The ringing in his ears fades as they wait, leaning slightly forward, but it doesn't go away. Barely heard, but still there.

"It's so strange," Lorna says and pushes her chair back. Phelien and Berthelen spring up, dropping their napkins from their laps. His so-called friends. *Huh.* He's barely seen them this summer. After the hair grew out all of a sudden, they just came around to watch him struggle with the brush — such an exotic tool. And since the Noise became strong enough for them to hear clearly, they've been totally thrilled. This freak-friend of theirs is an endless source of entertainment.

"Sit down." Lorna's mother says, but Lorna has already rushed to her feet and looks around suspiciously, her eyes finally landing on Sheyen.

"Could it be coming from outside?" Lorna asks.

Oh, for Salt's sake, playing ignorant just to call him out is an insult not only to him, but to Sediniel, to fucking Delyan too.

Sheyen keeps chewing his bream.

"Could there be something in the gardens?" Berthelen whispers to Lorna, leaning toward Sheyen. *Very funny, Berthelen. Yes, the In-Betweens are coming for you.*

"Come on, children, don't be silly," Lorna's mother says and turns back to her plate, her cheeks flushed. The ringing fades away completely. Sheyen hardly resists the urge to rub his ears — the others don't need more fuel.

"It was like the rumbling before an earthquake," Berthelen says, grasping for words, "But there was a high pitch to it too. It was like your gut clenching when you hear something been torn."

"Enough. This is nonsense," his omniscience, Delyan says, so nonsense it must be. Lorna's mother grants Delyan a nod and a prim smile. She gathers her shawl around her shoulders and clears her throat. *Nonsense, says Delyan Nedyre, first Artist of the Academy, so yes, let's keep eating fish.*

Berthelen is the last to sit back down. As he takes his seat by Sheyen, he leans over to leer and whisper, "Or maybe, it's an In-Between's squeal." The sun-glare glimmers on his bare pate.

Sheyen grips his fork and stabs the next bite, concentrates on how to swallow without choking.

"Let's make a toast," Delyan says and raises his glass. "To our Sediniel, who crossed into adulthood today. May your tattoos sway gently under the wind of the Art."

Glasses clink and Sheyen does not look any of them in the eye. Not even Sediniel, though he knows that's petty of him. He sips some wine; he can't allow himself to jinx her. It's supposed to be honeyed but it tastes like ash.

This, too, is in the book Sediniel hates. Whatever the In-Betweens eat tastes bitter, and they always crave something sweet. It could have been written about him, really, and he bets his friends read it too, so he drinks some more.

Delyan clears his throat. Sheyen can feel his father's eyes on him, but no, he won't look up; Mom is not here to scold him this time. Even Delyan didn't dare invite his exotic Caprishi mistress to a family party. Sheyen's presence was never questioned, since he used to look like the rest and Sediniel wouldn't have it otherwise, but things have changed and clearly, Delyan didn't realize how much.

"Also," Delyan says, "I am confident that next year Sheyen will also be ready to join the Academy." *Great, they're all staring now.* "To progress and advancement."

Sheyen finally looks up from the red algae garnish, his cheeks hot, his ears ringing. On his right, Berthelen stifles a giggle.

"Everyone gets in the Academy at fourteen," Sheyen says, gripping the glass he is not raising. What will he do if he's never accepted in the Academy? Become a sailor, like his mother? Work the salt marshes or the fields, like the Artless? Be exiled so that this weird Noise of his only echoes far from Vensymari ears, away from home? He tries hard not to blink as the rest of the company sits still, their glasses half raised, their hairless heads reflecting midday's sun-glare. The adults are polite enough to smile, but Lorna and Berthelen and Phelien stare, pressing their lips together to prevent a laugh.

"Sheyen, everyone's talent in the Art matures in its own pace. Yours is special." Delyan wears his disciplined tone, which says *be silent.*

"Special as in freakish," Berthelen mutters under his breath and Lorna leans forward to hide her smirk behind her woven fan.

"Perhaps what In-Betweens lack in talent, they make up for it in hair," she whispers loud enough for Sheyen to hear it. Sweat swells out of the roots of his hair and he wipes it with the back of his hand. How stupid of him to expect that things would remain the same after the hair grew out. At least Sediniel looks as pissed as he feels. She grips her fork so hard that her knuckles turn white while trying to pin down an olive and failing.

"Sediniel, your glass," her mother says, eyebrows arched and smiling.

"To the talented," Delyan says and faint clinking follows.

"And to the In-Betweens," Berthelen sniggers, elbowing Lorna under the table.

Sheyen does not dare to look at him, for fear he might plant a punch in Berthelen's throat. Sediniel fidgets as her fork screeches against the porcelain plate; the olive still rolling.

"Phelien, why don't you take Lorna and Berthelen for a walk?" This is Lorna's mother, and her voice carries an urgency that can't really be argued. All three of them push their chairs back and step out, humming the old In-Between nursery rhyme. *Halfwits.* He swallows; his ears pop. The ringing starts again. Only a month ago, all five of them would have run out together. How could he have ever thought that things would get better? He hoped the hair would be overlooked, that once he got in the Academy all would be disregarded, interpreted as a misunderstanding. Today is a nightmare.

The ringing in his ears reaches a high pitch, muffling all other sounds as if it presses a pillow against the world. Everyone winces at the Noise, hands fly up to ears; Delyan shoots him a sharp glance. Sediniel takes his hand in hers under the table and squeezes it.

Sheyen holds his breath, *stop*; the ringing blares. The air tastes metallic, specks of dust flood his throat, stick to his tongue. Sheyen swallows, his head light like a drifting bubble. What if they're right, what if the stories hold truth? What if he is turning into an In-Between after all? He pushes the chair back and starts running.

"Sheyen? Where are you going?"

As soon as he leaves the mansion, the ringing stops, his ears still throbbing, his brain numb. He walks across the saltwood garden, all the way to the cliffs overlooking an ashen sea, summer storm dawning over the horizon. He would be better off inside the mansion, only he isn't going back. Nobody will care if he misses dessert anyway, all of them too busy cooing over Sediniel's new tattoos. All of them ignoring that he also turned fourteen, months ago, and yet no tattoos for him.

A stick breaks underfoot and he turns to see Sediniel resting against a tree trunk, looking at him over an apple. The scarlet tattoos meander on the skin of her bare skull, under the shallow breath of the wind. They make her look like the rest of them, all grown up. Ready to harness her talent in the Art.

"You hate apples," his voice scratching his throat. "Just throw it away."

"Father says we shouldn't waste food —"

"It's not that he can't afford it."

He grabs the apple from her hand and makes a run for the edge of the gardens. Chest crashing into the iron balustrades, he tosses it down the cliff and watches it roll until it hits the rocks by the beach.

"Why did you do that?" Sediniel struggles to catch her breath as she sticks her face out of the rails, looking down.

"I just did you a favor. You are an adult now, anyway. You don't *have to* eat it," he says, with half an eye on her tattoos. "You're a full citizen."

He tries his foot on the railing, makes sure that it holds and climbs. The rust, eating away the metal, smudges his palms. Sediniel watches closely, the tattoos' brisk movement betraying her agitation.

"I, on the other hand, am obviously a child, so I can still do this, right?" He balances with a single foot on the railing. He shoots a grin her way, swift and sharp, to chop her gurgling disapproval at its root.

"Come with me. Look!" He lowers himself to ride the iron, one leg hanging out, and nods towards three distant figures walking along the beach. "It's Lorna and the others."

"So what? Come on, let's get back inside, there is a huge storm coming and Latima is making chocolate." She pulls his leg, almost hanging her whole weight on it.

"Let's go and say hi." His fists are itching for a brawl. "Stop it, let's go meet them. Stop!"

"No." She climbs up and grabs him by the hair. He pulls loose and loses his balance for good, landing on the other side of the fence, face down in the dirt.

The wind howls.

"And they made *you* an adult?" He springs up, readjusting his belt. There are twigs and grass tangled in his hair. Why couldn't he remain as he was, hairless like everyone else — except Mom? His eyes sting a bit, but nah, it's the wind.

Sediniel is still on the ground, on the other side, dusting off her cloak.

"I'm not going back inside." His gaze wanders to the beach below, the three silhouettes gone now. They must have taken the long route back to the mansion. So, they'd rather chance the grey cliffs in a storm than pass by him. Without a warning, as always, the ringing roars in his head, louder than ever, deafening. *Fine.*

"Sheyen? Do you hear the Noise? Sheyen?"

Let her talk and shout. It's all right, she's got to be mature now. He runs down the path towards the sea and the ringing runs along with him, piercing his brain, muffling his breathing, the sound of his steps. It brings with it the stark smell of ice, the tart taste of marmalade gone bad. He spits. His ears hurt. It feels like they're bleeding, but when he reaches the sea, the ringing stops, abruptly, absolutely.

As if a blade cut it in half.

Sheyen takes a sharp breath, his lungs hungry for air, like he's just barely escaped drowning. He looks over his shoulder. Back along the path, Sediniel's mouth opens and closes without a sound. *At a loss for words, huh?*

He takes his stand on the beach, a couple of pebbles in his hand. He takes his shoes off; the tingling of the cold water under his feet feels soothing. The cinnamon-sanded beach stretches long and narrow to either side, abandoned in acute silence. The storm approaches fast yet mute. No wind. No waves, which is rare. Even the neighbor's dogs have stopped barking. He sends the first pebble skimming across the surface, but it does not skip at all, just sinks.

He takes his shirt off, throws it towards his shoes, by a flat rock. The silver sails of Mom's ship are nowhere to be seen. She is always there to preach about taking pride in their Caprishi heritage — her heritage, only half his — but always gone when they give him trouble about it. He dares a step forward.

"Did you hear that?" Sediniel says behind him and he jumps.

"When did you... Hear what? The Noise?" He gapes at her as she looks around, her lips thin, her eyes squinting. Her shoes are already wet.

"Sssh!" She is walking on the tip of her toes, but the soft crunch of dried seaweed betrays her. Where was it before? Her long neck stretches as she tries to hear better, forehead furrowed and full of doubt.

"What is it? I don't hear anything."

"I think it was the Noise, but this time it sounded different. More like a screeching, or fabric being ripped." She pulls her tunic tight around her.

"Like a ringing perhaps?" he asks, "Or shrill, like the laughter of the In-Betweens?"

"No. Shut up, Sheyen. It's gone now anyway." She folds her hands on her chest, shuddering . He sits on the ground and takes another couple of pebbles in his hand.

"It never crossed your mind? That the tales might be true?" he asks. *"Cursed is who lies in-between, who sways back and forth, neither out nor in. Hunted by those who spot the sign, its mane, its ear, its mismatched eye? They say it of all the half-breeds."*

"It's about the In-Betweens, not about half-Vensymari children," she scoffs.

"Oh really? Well, that's the song Phelien and Berthelen were humming at lunch. *Haunted by both silence and noise, torn between a home and a choice. Damned to belong under the frames of doors that lead to opposite ways. Cursed is who lies in-between, not one of us, a soul incomp—"*

"Stop it! And no, only the illiterate believe in old-wives tales."

"The stories say that all they can taste is bitterness! My tongue doesn't feel right today. They just linger in this In-Between place because they have nowhere else to go. And they won't let me into the Academy. Dina, what if it's happening?"

"You're just scared."

She kneels next to him and palms a pebble herself, weighs it and then throws it as far as she can.

Not a sound comes back.

"What's the Noise like for you?" he asks. "When it comes, I can only hear this damned ringing in my ears. The others said that it sounds like a rumbling and at the same time like paper being torn." His voice comes out almost too loud.

"Who said that?"

"Lorna, Berthelen, Phelien, everyone."

"They're idiots," she snaps. She flicks the pebble and then another and another. None skips. "They have no right to treat you like that," her voice an imitation of her mother's. She flicks and flicks as if her only goal in the entire world is to empty this shore of its pebbles. "You're my brother and th—"

"Don't!" He grabs her arm and looks around.

"Why not? It's not a damned secret."

"No? Then why am I not called Nedyre, like you? Why did I not get any tattoos? Delyan's other sons all had them at my age."

She twitches, opens her mouth, but stays mute.

Sheyen lets go of her. The tips of her ears are red, like always when she's angry. His cheeks are burning.

A drop of rain lands on the naked skin of her head, then another and another. And then, he notices. Her tattoos have lost their brightness, their color only a muted shade of red.

"Put your hood up," he says in a careful voice. "Are you feeling all right?" Her tattoos stop swaying. They're not supposed to do that. He runs his tongue over his lips. They taste like a stranger's — like porcelain, unused and undusted.

"It's so quiet," she whispers.

Plump drops of chilly rain land heavy on his cheeks. He blinks hard, chasing the swelling tears away as he stands, letting her expression sink in behind his eyes, in silence. This silence they share and this Noise they don't.

Sediniel suddenly looks back, towards the mansion, rainwater racing unhindered down her nape, soaking her light green tunic.

"Tell me what you heard before. I need to know," Sheyen says.

"No."

"Why not?"

Her nails must be down to the roots the way she is biting them now.

"Was it that horrible?" he asks.

Lightning. *Nine woven blossoms, eight woven blossoms, seven woven blossoms.* But no thunder.

"Yes. Like flesh being torn."

The rain raps against the rocks. The wind swoops in and he gasps as tiny needles prickle his skin, reaching deep to his lungs. Something is missing from the landscape, but he cannot tell what. He bends down to get his shirt and shoes, which lie drenched near her half-eaten apple.

The sounds. The sounds are missing.

"Leave it. Let's go."

"Sediniel, I need a favor."

"What?"

"It's the hair on my head. That's what's making the noise."

"That's about the stupidest thing I—"

"No, think. The Noise started when the hair appeared. And it's getting worse every day. And if there is any truth in the stories, we must stop it. What if my eyes are next? What if I wake up and one of them is suddenly blue, or brown or anything other than green? What if I drag you to the In-Between place?"

Lightning.

"I need to shave it off. I don't care if Mom gets angry or disowns me or lectures me forever. She's not mixed. She's just foreign. I should have got rid of the stupid hair a month ago."

"It's illegal to shave it. You're not a Vensymari to go around bald, you need to get approval first," she says in one breath, looking at him straight in the eye.

"I'm the First Artist's son, right? They won't do shit to me."

Sediniel scans the beach, her gaze travelling from his clothes up to the garden and then to the clouds. "Something feels wrong. I feel like... like I'm standing at the edge of a cliff. It's weird out here; too quiet."

"That's what I'm saying," he shouts. "It's happening and we have to stop it. Will you help me get rid of the hair?"

Mute lightning flashes. A wave swells and crashes against the rocks without a sound. Sediniel presses her lips together and holds her breath. Rain drenches her in silence.

"Fine." Her eyes linger on the soundless waves. "But only if you come back to the house with me. Now."

Sheyen nods, relief spreading on his shoulder blades like warm butter. "We'll sneak in through the kitchen so nobody sees."

They run back, Sediniel first with Sheyen lagging behind her to steal a last glance at the wrinkled sea; Mom had better be back soon.

The mansion, their father's summer home, always smells of baking. Its thick stone walls, its light elderberry furniture, the curtains, the sheets and the inside of the wardrobes, have all been imbued with the fragrance of dessert cooking in the ovens. Today, it's lemongrass pie and hot caramel-flavored chocolate. The smell spreads better in the silence.

Only it shouldn't be silent. Their father should be here, sipping seadrop liquor with their friends' parents by the unlit fireplace. When he left, they were all still lounging in the dining room, heavy with Latima's cooking. He can't hear them now; even the servants are nowhere to be seen.

Still shivering, barefoot and half-naked, he crouches over the boiling pot of chocolate, letting the delicious steam warm his insides. The thought of grabbing a spoon and digging in flashes, then fades.

"Hello?" Sediniel almost whispers standing under the doorframe, looking down the drab corridor. She trails back into the kitchen and closes the door gently behind her, heading for the saltwood chest where a blunt pair of scissors is kept under the towels. The water-weight clock that never worked properly hangs overhead. The faint creaking of its cogs always out of tune, a tick too late, a tack too long. Only now it echoes smoothly, first a tick and then a tack, tick tack, tick tack.

"The clock is working," she mumbles distracted, groping in the chest.

It sounds wrong, he wants to tell her. Disorienting. But the words snag on his tongue.

"Where is everyone?" she asks and Sheyen turns to check the door they snuck in from, scanning the garden through its colored glass, hoping to spot someone they missed before.

"Perhaps they're out for a walk?" Alarm coils under her casual concern; her gaze has followed his.

"Could be."

"And Latima? The kitchen servants?"

"They're probably running some errands downtown." Highly unlikely, but she mustn't be sidetracked from the haircut, the moment is too convenient. What if she changes her mind? He's been nagging her to help him for a month now, and she always refused.

"All four of them?" Sediniel strokes her head just above the forehead, her tattoos still dim and lifeless, but she doesn't seem to notice and he won't tell. He glances at the scissors.

Lightning. Unheard thunder rattles the pots on their shelf.

"Something is wrong," mutters Sediniel darting glances at the shelves as if they are about to tilt and crack. "The house is wrong, they didn't even put out the ovens. And the storm," Sediniel says pointing a finger towards the glass door. Rain whips the glass and for a couple of breaths they linger, waiting for the din to come; what comes is only silence.

She approaches the door, ready to open it.

"Sediniel?" he says. "Quit stalling. Obviously, they're going to be back any minute now. We need to be quick."

"Quick? Sheyen, something is off, I can't hear a thing from outside the house. No rain, no thunder, no barking dogs. Nothing."

"I know, which is why we should do it now. Something's happening to me and maybe this is how we stop it."

"Why would it stop? And not a word about the stupid tales." Her face is taut, about to snap, her lips a line, her fists bunched. "There is no such thing as... as the In-Between People." Finally, *finally* she turns away from the door. "But, if that's what you want... When your mother comes back though, you won't hear the end of it." Reaching into the top drawer, she pulls out a small bundle wrapped in the scraps of old kitchen towels.

"Latima's meat razors," she whispers in answer to his arched eyebrows.

The razors rattle as they land on the table by the scissors. Sediniel crouches over the thin blades, inspecting them closely and takes one between thumb and finger.

"I'm not sure how to use these, I might cut you."

"I don't mind, just do it." But she's not listening. Sheyen follows her unflinching look which turns towards the glass door.

Three figures stand there, waving, drenched.

"It's the others," Sheyen says. He wants to move but for a couple of deafening heartbeats his feet are wreathed with iron. The figures' gestures expand, become quick, become sharp. Yet there is no sound as their fists pound the glass. Before thoughts form, he rushes to the glass door to latch it shut.

"Sheyen," Sediniel gasps but Berthelen is already leaning against the glass and turning the door-knob. He takes a step into the kitchen. The water-weight clock sounds a bell and stops.

The room seems smaller with all three of them bursting inside. Berthelen's shoulders have widened over the summer and he now stands a full head taller than Sheyen. Drops of rain gleam faintly on the skin of his head, and his hands are curled into fists by his sides, face washed red with anger. Lorna stands next to him, skinny and poised. She pushes her hood back tossing unreadable looks to her older brother, Phelien, who looms behind them. Sheyen doesn't like the way he unfolds his Vensymari limbs, long, lithe, and braided with muscle. Sheyen struggles not to take a step back. This is, after all, his house.

Scurrying feet tap on the marble and Sediniel stops next to him. He turns and looks and his heart skips a beat. She is scared.

"What's wrong? What happened to your tattoos?" she says.

"Same that happened to yours," Phelien growls.

"What?" She whips around and her eyes lash at Sheyen for confirmation. Her hand flies up to her skull, fingers tracing the fading patterns. Sheyen returns the stare and nods slightly. It's pointless to lie. "This can't be happening." She tries to catch a glimpse of her reflection in the glass.

"Something's terribly wrong." Lorna's crystal pitched voice, now so cold and clear. No one moves. Not right away. Then, Phelien takes a step forward, heads for the chair closest to the kitchen bench and sits, carefully, scanning the room as if looking for something stolen.

"The sounds outside are missing. Everyone else is missing," he says. "It's just us."

"We came back from the beach and no one was home," Lorna says, like crystal cracking. As she opens her mouth to speak again, Sheyen feels his hair stand on end.

"Maybe they're out somewhere," Sediniel speaks first.

"No. We were just out looking for them. Not a soul." That's Berthelen. He is looking Sheyen straight in the eye. "We warned you."

Sheyen feels something creeping up the back of his throat, bile. His stomach is a tight knot that presses his chest, presses and presses. A sour taste in his mouth. He needs to run, only he won't.

"What? Are you serious?"

"The Noise took them. He took them. He's an In-Between." Lorna's voice comes out flat.

"Sheyen was with me all day, he didn't do anything. How could he, how could anyone? Are you stupid, did you hit your head on something?" Sediniel has taken her place right in front of him.

"Cut it off, Sediniel. You've heard the Noise inside him. He sent them to the In-Between place, because he hates them all."

Time is a drowsy cat arching its back slowly. Lorna looks so different now that Sheyen realizes that he doesn't really know her. Not the girl he played tag with;

when they ran until their lungs were about to burst, stumbled on a root and feigned falling and then kissed, a swift brush of lips against lips followed by secret smiles and a prickly sensation running right under his skin.

"How would he do that?" Sediniel roars. "How—"

"Shut your mouth." Phelien stands up, arms ready to strike.

"You shut up, you rotten pigfly shit," Sheyen pushes his sister aside and walks up to Phelien. A blow just under his ribs might be enough to force him down, if he moves fast.

Berthelen jumps Sheyen from behind; he falls on Sheyen hard, knocking him flat on the marble. Before Sheyen can crawl back up, Berthelen sits on his waist, knees on his sides squeezing tight, pinning him, face down.

"Stop it, you tarnished half-breed," Berthelen says. "Bring them back!" He grabs Sheyen by the hair and pulls up so hard that Sheyen hears a loud crack at the base of his neck. Berthelen loosens his grip, but, as Sheyen's still pinned down, there's little he can do. He squirms, growls and gasps.

"Stop! What are you doing?" Sediniel's voice pierces Sheyen's ears and only now he realizes she's been going like that for some time.

"Bring them back!" Berthelen leans close to his ear and shouts as if he's about to spit his lungs out.

"Just a minute, and I'll fart them out." Sheyen snorts. He would sneer but he feels the skin of his face stretched tight on his cheekbones.

"Bring them back, you soulless mutt."

"It's the hair. Get rid of it. Make it stop," Lorna shouts.

"I'll do it!" Sediniel's voice comes out strained, almost choked. "Let me do it! We were about to cut his hair anyway." She brandishes the razors and the scissors, Phelien steps back. "That's what he wanted me to do. Right, Sheyen?"

He can barely turn his head to see her. He wanted to get rid of the stain, true enough, but this stain, he now sees, will never leave. It has spread, quick as ink on white linen. Blending in is not going to happen. The tattoos are not going to happen. Kissing Lorna again is not going to happen.

"Fuck her." Lorna is standing by the boiling chocolate pot. "Cutting it is not enough. Let's burn it off him. Make sure it never grows again."

Sheyen's mouth turns numb, his tongue a sack of sand about to crumble.

"Hold him tight," Phelien barks. Sheyen gulps down air too thin to fill his lungs.

"You've gone mad," Sediniel hisses, close by, on his right. Berthelen ignores her, digs his knees deeper under Sheyen's ribs, making him wince and writhe. Metal clatters; Lorna gasps.

Now. Sediniel releases a holler. She charges at Berthelen, pouncing on him like a rabid dog. Berthelen screams and loses his grip. Muscles bowstring taut, veins sizzling with panic, Sheyen rolls over and pushes himself up. He lunges at Phelien and Lorna and thrusts at the pot they're holding. Metal clanks and Phelien shrieks as the pot lands on his toes; boiling chocolate spills over his arms, feet and clothes, quickly spreading on the floor. Phelien stumbles back, eyes wild, scalded arms flopping.

Sheyen whips around to check on Sediniel, sprawled in the corner by the glass door, lips bleeding. Berthelen marches towards her. Sheyen thrusts at Berthelen to push him aside. Sediniel launches first, razors in hand, before

Berthelen's foot digs into her groin sending her crawling. Sheyen clashes into him and shoves him aside, hard. He sweeps to his sister, razors scattered on the soiled boards. Lightning. Her eyes swell with angry tears, her jaw fixed tight. He props her up and together they rush to the glass door.

The door behind them stands ajar while they pant their way through the garden. There is no denying it now; the world outside the house has been stripped of every sound, an animated painting raging around them. The rain pours down mute and cold, turning the soil to mud; the leaves shake on the saltwood trees without a rustle.

"Run." He drags her on until they reach the fence where they climb over, supporting each other, limbs shaky. They careen down the path to the beach.

"We need to get away from the house," his voice hoarse. The pebbles churn under their feet as they reach the rocks just above the water and stop.

A slurping sound ripples the silence. The sound of flesh breaking. The rumbling of a mouth full of stones. A high pitched screeching. *So that's how it sounds.*

"The Noise," Sediniel whispers.

A hunched figure stands on the spot where Sheyen's clothes should be, by the rocks. No taller than he, dressed in his shirt, wearing his shoes, lank golden hair hanging drenched to its ankles. Bony tattooed hands huddled up to its chest, clenching the discarded apple. The figure sups its juice, swallows and buries its face in the fruit, gnawing, lips pulled back; there are no teeth, just gums. It sucks and swallows and never looks up, famished. The Noise emanates from inside it, growing louder with every chunk it gobbles.

Sheyen takes his sister's hand and gently pulls her closer, her breath rasping in his ear. The creature stands just steps away from them. Sheyen can't bear to look at its face. The creature smacks its lips, sucks at its gums and stumbles forward.

They don't wait for it to take a second step. Faster than their racing heartbeats, they turn together and, holding hands, they jump into the sea, falling among the soundless raindrops for a panicked eternity before they hit the surface. Coming up for air, looking at each other, they start swimming away from the beach as fast as they can. The waves rage bitter and silent, salt creeping in the wounds of his chapped lips. Sediniel pushes him on, stroke after stroke leaving them in the exact same spot with backs turned to the house until a drop of courage forces him to look over his shoulder.

"Look," he says.

The figure, a white smudge in the dark, dawdles up the path they came from. Sheyen can hardly hear the Noise from this far. It reaches the fence and climbs over. It keeps walking, through the garden towards the kitchen. Towards the door that's left ajar. Towards the others.

Shivers seize him. Lightning. The creature stumbles into the kitchen. Nine woven blossoms, eight woven blossoms, seven woven blossoms. Screams, and then nothing. Only silence. The house falls dark.

Suddenly thunder. The wind now blusters and the rain splashes around them.

"Sheyen," Sediniel gasps. It's the house, all lit up now, not just the kitchen. There are figures in the garden and along the path to the beach, holding lanterns. Voices. Familiar. They call their names. Their father.

Sediniel pulls him first towards the shore, pushing his limp body to swim.

When their feet touch the sand, she hugs him. Her tattoos glisten red under the faint moonlight.

"I see them," Latima shouts, "Delyan! I see them!"

The beach feels frozen as they crawl out. Warm arms wrap around them. Their father's face looks strange, stripped as it were of color.

"Where were you?" Latima has run down with blankets. "We've been waiting in the house, thinking you would be back by nightfall," she stifles a sob. "We've looked for you everywhere."

"Where were you? Sheyen?" Their father rubs his arms to warm him; Latima is cradling Sediniel. Limbs limp, Sheyen stares back through tangled hair.

"You're bruised!" His voice frays. "Sheyen, what happened?" He shakes him hard. "Where are the others? Were you together?"

He sees them now, the parents of Lorna and Berthelen and Phelien, lanterns in their hands, their eyes wild as they search for those who are not there.

"Where are they?" his father asks again.

Sheyen turns his head towards his sister, licks his lips — they're sore.

Sediniel nods slowly. Licks the tears that reach down to the corners of her mouth. Sheyen seals his lips shut. He rubs the lobes of his ears; for now, it's quiet inside him.

See Vaya Pseftaki's story "The Noise Inside" online at Metaphorosis.
If you liked it, leave a comment. Authors love that!
Remember to subscribe to our e-mail updates so you'll know when new stories are posted.

About the story

The idea of a strange noise emanating from someone emerged as I was struggling with Julia Kristeva's *Powers of Horror*. Around that time, I was also playing in a D&D campaign based on Fritz Leiber's Lankhmar books. This unholy combination produced the character of Sheyen, who, in the process of the story, mutated and bloomed. Kristeva's theory of Abjection played a subliminal role in the process of world-building, and especially in the conception of the liminal In-Betweens, pushing the narrative deeper into a subtle horror atmosphere. As a non-binary person myself, the concept of the In-Betweens hit a nerve and thus, before I even realized it, the whole story was built around what it means to never be sure where you belong to, and the horror that ensues. Despite the fact that the first draft of the story finished in 2015, it took me three full years to shape it into a cohesive narrative. At first it spilled out raw, unprocessed; it felt almost like a throbbing wound. It had hit close to home, and thus I found myself unable to touch it. I could tell that it could be explored and crafted into a narrative that made sense to others too, but what I didn't realize back then was that it would be such a long process. Other stories went by, some of them got published, but my mind kept going back to this incomplete piece. Three years later, I was offered the opportunity to work on it again. Even after all this time, editing and re-writing posed a challenge. Luckily, now, I was armed with the nerve needed to spin it right.

A question for the author

Q: If you could have a meal with a character from any classic novel, whom would you choose?

A: I would gladly take Basil Hallward, the painter from *The Picture of Dorian Gray*, out to dinner. Though overshadowed by the dashing Dorian, he is the most tragic figure in the book; his unrequited love morphs into a literal window to hell. To top it all, he ends up being murdered. The check would definitely be on me, along with plenty of shots.

About the author

Vaya Pseftaki is a writer, translator, creative writing teacher and RPG maniac. They are usually found sipping coffee from bottomless cups and watching bug documentaries. Their fiction can be found either in Greek or in English in various venues. They currently live in Thessaloniki, Greece, trying to train fleas to do their bidding.

@Vaya_Pseftaki

L'Appel du Vide

Rajiv Moté

On Friday morning, the ambient heaviness in his boss's tiny office threatened to bend Isaac double, and his ears ached from the pressure in the air. The dread hadn't started with his boss's unexpected meeting request, but coalesced around it, wrapping the 15-minute block on his calendar in layers of doubt and worry until it shone like a fat, anxious pearl. It had been gathering over weeks. Office doors that usually stayed open were shut. Hallways and corners sheltered low, furtive conversations; Isaac felt like he was interrupting conspiracies every time he walked to the restroom. The very air resisted movement, its weight dragging down shoulders and gazes. It felt like the air before a storm cracks open the sky.

His boss, from across the desk, began by telling him what Isaac already knew.

"As you know…"

A disappointing Q2. A gloomy forecast for Q3. Streamlining. Tightening belts. Pivoting. Reorganizing. Isaac waited as each term in the well-rehearsed speech pulled him in, spiraling closer to the actual point.

"We have to let you go."

There. The dice showed their pips. The curtain pulled back. With the word "go," Isaac was unmoored. First, figuratively, and then, a heartbeat later, literally. His boss was still talking while Isaac floated inches above his seat. He panicked for a moment, losing the leverage that came with gravity. Putting his feet back on the floor only pushed him up higher, until he was floating in the middle of the room. He began to tilt, and his arms and legs flailed for some kind of purchase. His boss's eyes held polite sympathy. He asked if Isaac had any questions. Isaac shook his head. In his flailing, he found he could change his orientation and even propel himself by pushing against the thickened air.

"Your belongings will be shipped to your home," his boss said, "so I'm going to ask that you leave the office now. This will be a difficult day here, and I'd appreciate if you helped minimize the distractions."

Experimentally, Isaac tucked his knees into his chest and flapped his arms.

"Do you need some help with the door?"

Isaac executed a slow, controlled roll in mid-air. As he faced the door, upside down, he took the opportunity to turn the knob and open it. "No," he said, keeping the emotion out of his voice. "I'm good." With a kick of his legs, he floated out among the cubicles.

"I'm out of a job," Isaac said, low enough for his own ears only, to confirm what his brain had only begun to process. He knew the danger of the ground falling out from under one's feet, the sensation of endlessly falling. It had happened a lot in the neighborhood where he grew up. Folks with no plan and no place to go, floating down the street or hovering over the corner, their arms and legs windmilling to stay upright. A strong wind could blow them away. Gone. Mama wouldn't have any of that from her boys. The moment he or his brother Ray started to rise an inch or two off the floor, she would pull them back down and stick their noses into a school book. Their mama said that the day their father walked out on them, he fell straight up into the air and probably burned himself to a crisp in the sun, good riddance to the man. Real men could be counted on to keep their feet on the ground.

Viewed from above, the rows of cubes looked small and orderly, the sense of sameness and pattern overwhelming people's attempts to stamp them with individual personalities. His colleagues—ex-colleagues—glanced up as he passed over them, but no more than glanced, as if the strain of lifting their eyes above their screens were too great in this heavy air. There was envy in some of those glances. 'Oh, this looks fun?' Isaac thought. 'See how fun it is when you can't stand up.'

He drifted over his own cube. On the desk were the computer and phone, which belonged to the company. A stack of papers he'd someday hoped to sort. A tiny dead cactus in a pot. Pens, notepads, a mug, a water bottle—all with the company logo. Relics. He was swimming over the sunken ruins of his last seven-odd years. There was also a framed picture of Tonya and the girls, Janae and Krista, ages seven and five. Tonya crouched behind the two girls, her hands around their shoulders. He called them his inspiration, the reason he was here. All three smiled wide, brilliant smiles, polished to a gleam by his employer-subsidized dental insurance.

"Good morning, ladies," he said, stretching his arm, reaching for the picture. All three beamed back. "I've got news. It's... not so good." Their big brown eyes were full of expectation. "But it'll wait."

Reaching far enough to strain his shoulder, he grasped the picture and traced the simulated grain of the fake wood frame with his fingertips. It was the only thing he managed to grab, but it was all he needed to take with him. He knew there were things down in the drawers too, but they were mostly what he put there without any intention of retrieving. Vendor swag, business cards, the employee handbook. He didn't need any of it anymore. He had never needed it. It was strange—all those hours here, and so little to mark his time.

"Hey man," Andre called to him on the way back from filling his coffee mug. "Moving up, I see."

"Yeah," Isaac said. "But not here."

Andre nodded, his expression becoming interested. "So it's begun, huh?" Andre had his ear to the company grapevine, and had guessed the reason behind the change in atmosphere. He called himself the Weatherman, because he knew which way the wind would blow.

Isaac nodded back, treading air. "You were right." It was strange to look down on Andre, who was a head taller than him.

Andre sighed. "Okay. Well. I'm not going say sorry, I'm going to say congratulations. Onward and upward. Good luck with whatever's next. And keep in touch, all right? Wherever you land, keep me in mind. I'll bet this is not over yet."

"Will do. Best of luck, man." The thought of landing was bleak. It felt as unreachable as the junk in his desk drawer. With a kick, he propelled himself down a hallway and through the break room, toward the exit. He avoided conversation, 'to minimize the distraction on this difficult day,' but he smiled and waved to former colleagues as he passed above them. Somehow, the smiles came easily. The work, follow-ups, and replies he owed several of them just weren't his problem anymore. There were nice reasons to lose touch with the ground too, at least for a while. First love could do it. Winning a scholarship. Getting the kind of job that had a real future. Isaac knew guys who came back from time served and didn't touch the ground for weeks until the old drama of the neighborhood got its hooks back in. Maybe this was what freedom felt like. His thumb stroked the plastic picture frame. Maybe this was how his father felt when he disappeared into the sky.

He realized what he must look like, floating to the lobby doors, smiling like a fool. He put on a serious expression, the expression of a man who understood the gravity of his situation and was carefully considering his next move. But his feet didn't quite touch the floor the way a man's did when he was carrying around serious thoughts. He was literally buoyant.

Not trusting the physics of weightlessness in an elevator, he took the stairs down the 14 floors to the lobby. He drifted on his belly down the stairwell, like a skydiver before the parachute opens. With nobody watching, he allowed himself a laugh. He added some flourishes, rotating his body like a drill, corkscrewing down the spiral. In the privacy of the stairwell, he felt more like a superhero than a man who had just lost the means to support his family. Then he had an idea —a crazy one—and he reversed direction. With a kick off the railing, he rose, up past the 14th floor, up to the 25th, where he touched the carpet only long enough to open the door to the rooftop deck.

It was June, and the lawn chairs and enormous shade umbrellas were out. People on their breaks, enjoying the sun and the view, turned when Isaac floated out onto the deck. "Well good for you," a woman said to him, and a young guy gave him a thumbs up. Maybe they thought he'd fallen in love. He hovered just above the high concrete railing and looked down. The wind was strong up here, but he wasn't completely unanchored. The smiling family in the picture frame he held kept him from getting too carried away. Below, the cabs, buses, and trucks on Jackson Boulevard jockeyed for position among the lanes, and people walked along the sidewalks, jaywalking when the lights turned red. There was a hum below that Isaac always liked.

It had been a dream of Isaac's to work downtown, amidst that bustle. That's what he had grown up thinking success looked like. Success was a destination, and he'd made it, against the odds. He'd done what was needed. The next pieces of his life had fallen into place more easily than he could believe. He'd earned promotions, gotten married, had kids, and even bought a house in a nice neighborhood.

But he was embarrassed to realize he hadn't given much thought to what made up the hours of daily life leading to that success. What occupied those hours was... hard to describe. He had a vague, jumbled impression of email, to-do lists, meetings, reports, whiteboards, spreadsheets, jargon, and coffee. It was a mire of busyness that spanned more than ten years and three companies, and every day he sank deeper. He didn't want to be ungrateful, but he'd lost track of the 'why.' His daughter Janae once asked him what his work was for, and he realized he didn't even know anymore.

Isaac glanced down at the framed photograph in his hands, and took a deep breath. It was heavier than it should have been, for wood-colored plastic. Soon, he'd have to deal with what would be next. He'd have to sell himself. The thought was heavier than the frame. But it didn't have to be right now. Not just this moment. Surely he'd earned a little fun on the way back down. He pushed against the air, moving out over Jackson Boulevard, 25 floors below. Slowly, like a bead sinking in honey, he descended. He gave a few kicks to make sure he could regain height, but once he was satisfied, he allowed gravity to exert its weakened pull and just enjoyed the sensation of floating.

He'd explored downtown longer than the decade he worked here, but he'd never seen it like this. In the corners outside windows he saw big spiders in their webs, anchored against the wind. He passed pigeons roosting on ledges, and even a falcon, considering which of the pigeons to murder. He sank past windows of offices and conference rooms, and waved on the way down. Some waved back. Others did their best to ignore him.

"Isaac!" called a voice. "Hey, man, come down!"

Ten floors below, on the sidewalk outside his ex-building's main lobby, Andre was calling up to him.

Isaac aimed himself and scooped at the air to descend faster. He stopped just short of the ground, hovering at eye level with Andre. He didn't let his feet touch down, for fear that he wouldn't rise again.

"They got me right after you," Andre said. "My boss didn't even put anything on the calendar. Complete drive-by. I hate being right all the time."

"Well, you're the Weatherman. I'm sorry. Or congratulations, if that's how you feel. So it's a bloodbath in there?" Isaac tried to sound sympathetic. Andre's feet were firmly on the ground.

"Yeah. I've heard of half a dozen, personally, but it's happening all through the company. I'm getting texts every fifteen minutes."

"So, are you going to... take some time?" Isaac liked Andre, but he didn't want to get pulled into the drama when he could be soaring among the buildings, examining mouldings and facades, and seeing everything from a new perspective. He'd earned this time to float free from the needs and expectations of others.

"That's why I called you down. I was talking to Samir, and it turns out he has some connections through a cousin. How would you like to work for our top competitor?" Andre bounced his eyebrows like he'd said something delightful and wicked.

Isaac dropped a couple of inches before he caught himself. "Doing what?"

"The same thing! Only for about $10K more, is what I'm hearing. Samir says he'll put in a word for both of us, but we have to move fast. Like you said, it was a bloodbath. We'll have competition."

Isaac felt gravity like a heavy cable reeling him back to earth. The picture frame in his hands was a lead weight. He kicked and waved his arms against the pull. It was all he could do to stay aloft.

"I get it, man," Andre said. "You just got kicked in the junk by a place you gave —what—five years? Take some time. Give yourself a start date a couple of weeks out. But don't give up on your passion because you got knocked down. You can't pass this up."

"Seven years." Isaac's toes brushed the concrete. Ten thousand dollars more. For whatever it was he did.

Their CEO had had a pep talk. 'If you're not passionate about what you do,' he'd say, 'then why are you even here?' Isaac didn't dare admit that in almost 12 years of professional life, he hadn't found a passion. But he could navigate an office, speak the jargon, follow process, and do things that brought modest, but not insignificant, increases to his paycheck every year. Tonya, Janae, and Krista smiled up at him from the picture in his hands. Maybe he had a passion for providing for his family. Taking Samir's job was the sensible thing to do. The safe thing. It was an unexpected lifeline in a sea of doubt. He ought to be grateful. It wasn't as if he had any other plan.

But the sky above, between the tall buildings, was the watercolor blue of early summer. He might never see it from up high again.

"I'm going to pass."

The words just came out, and before he could take them back, he felt a slack in the invisible cable tethering him. He pushed, and reclaimed a couple of inches of altitude. "I don't want to do this anymore." He was a head above Andre now. He caught a breeze.

"But what will you do, then?"

Isaac tried to think of an answer that sounded legitimate and responsible. Something that would describe a respectable place for him in the world as a contributor to his family, a provider for his kids. Something that wouldn't reveal just how much he was adrift. You can take the kid out of the 'hood...

"I have no idea," he finally said. More slack. Andre craned his neck to look up at him. "But I can't go back down there..."

Isaac rose like a party balloon with a cut string. As Andre became small and indistinguishable from the rest of the working crowd downtown, Isaac rode the wind, banking between buildings and circling landmarks laid out below him. At this height, the noise of the city was drowned out by the rush of air past his ears. Nobody could touch him here. Nobody could reach him. City blocks become patterns of multicolored geometry. Downtown became a cluster of tall buildings in a much larger city that hugged the lake, sprawling north, south, and west. And beyond it lay green, brown, and yellow rectangles of farms and prairie, crossed by ribbons of road and river, winding beyond sight even from this vantage. The world was vast. The world was very small.

Isaac shivered as he rose straight through a cumulus cloud. Breaking through to the top, he paused, momentarily blinded by the dazzling rainbow of diffracted sunlight, so bright the very air seemed to shine. Fluffy white islands drifted in the blue sky. He floated above a moderate-sized hill among dramatic cloud mountains, towers, and valleys, all shining white and pristine. The air was cold, but invigorating. He felt it entering and exiting his lungs, and his every sense felt sharp and alive.

Something whooshed past him with a cry of "Cannonball!" Isaac was horrified to see a person-shaped hole in the clouds beneath him. He let himself drop near the edge of the hole and peered down. Whoever had fallen was coming back up. He saw the red top of a knit winter hat rising toward him, with arms and legs below moving in a butterfly stroke. A shaggy-haired guy in a ski vest burst through the hole and let out a whoop.

"More like a belly flop, huh?" the man said as he rose alongside a fluffy plume of cloud.

Now that Isaac looked, he saw more people among the cumulus formations. Another man, this one in a suit and tie flapping in the wind, leaped from the top of the plume, executing a swan dive into the cloud. Others swam in and out of the cottony fluff, or snoozed in the sunlight. One was drifting on her back, reading a hardcover book. The realization jolted Isaac like a Monday alarm at 5 A.M. This was a thing. People lived like this. He didn't know whether to be astounded or furious.

Well he was here now. Isaac pushed off in pursuit of the shaggy man, spiraling up the plume. "Hey!" he called. "Hi!"

Shaggy paused, treading air for Isaac to catch up. "How's it going?" he called back.

"I had no idea about all this," Isaac said. "Is it... Is it always like this?"

Shaggy laughed. "New, huh?"

"I was laid off this morning."

Shaggy grinned with genuine enthusiasm. "Congratulations! Nice to be free, isn't it?"

Free? Isaac's eyes darted around the shining landscape as he was seized by the wild terror that he would see his father here, kicking back on a cloud. He kicked to regain some height. "It's something, alright."

Shaggy, whose name was actually Greg, introduced him to some of the other plume-divers. Most were regulars, and knew each other. They had a friendly competition going. Greg explained that to get any real speed, you needed to think of something that attached you 'to the world down there.' Obligations. Responsibilities. Something that really pulled at you. You dove, and at the last moment, you released it. And back up you went. "You want to try?"

The sun was just above the cloud line in the west. He'd have to go home soon. Go home and tell his family what had happened, and what he meant to do about it.

"Why not?" Isaac said.

He hovered above the tip of the plume and then raised the picture of Tonya, Janae, and Krista to his eyes. He said their names. He felt a tug somewhere in his gut. And then, before he could decide how to dive, he dropped like a stone. Isaac screamed. He heard a thin shout from above, nearly drowned out by the wind. "Just let go!"

No. His fingers clamped down on the plastic picture frame as he plummeted. 'No way in hell,' he thought. He wasn't like any of those people up playing in the clouds, privileged, without responsibilities, without a care in the world. He wasn't like those people in his old neighborhood, weighed down but still drifting. And he wasn't like his father. He had something besides himself to live and work for. He had a family. Something he'd die for.

'A fat lot of good that'll do us,' Tonya would have said. He looked down at the picture. The girls were still smiling, but Tonya was looking right at him, arching one eyebrow the way she did when she was done tolerating nonsense. Sometimes she used that eyebrow when telling him what he already knew—but she decided he needed to hear again. Things like 'If you don't want to be your father, then make a different choice. Be there for us. Be there for you.'

Isaac's fall slowed. She was right, of course. It wasn't his family weighing him down. He'd chosen what kind of man he wanted to be long ago. But that choice had gotten tangled up in the other things he thought he had to do. The mire that had slowly sucked him lower for years. Well, he was out of the mire now. Cut loose. So what next?

He realized he was no longer falling. The world was laid out before him, but the faces of Janae and Krista in the frame held his eyes. They were older now than when the photograph was taken, and even in Krista he saw glimmers of the women they'd become. They were more confident than he had been at that age. They laughed easier. They didn't live in fear of disappointing a parent who was embittered by loss, who never stopped working and never failed to remind her kids it was all for them. His kids were different. And he was different from his parents, either one.

He began to rise again. He rose, faster, and faster still. He wanted to fly. He needed to. He broke through the cloud plume and zoomed past Greg and the divers. He wasn't slowing down. At a certain height, rising became indistinguishable from falling. The air turned cold, thin, and weightless. The further he rose from the Earth, the less pull it exerted. Already the curve of the western horizon glowed crimson as the speck where he lived and once worked, far below, passed into the shadow of early evening.

The unobstructed night sky yawned above. What had started as black with a few pinpricks of light became a luminous river of heavenly bodies, from dust to planets, all reflecting the starshine. At the very precipice of the celestial chasm, everything seemed to fall away but what he chose to hold on to, like the picture frame that tethered him to a home in a nice neighborhood far below. Isaac stopped to take it all in. The emptiness had a pull of its own. All that space, never to be filled. He could imagine surrendering to the illuminated infinity, as easy as falling. It was thrilling in the way looking out over any beckoning abyss thrilled, as long as you trusted your anchor.

Isaac stretched his arms and legs wide, as if to embrace it all. He felt the cracks and pops as he stretched his neck and arched his back. His heart pounded. Blood roared in his ears. Nerves fired and flared like the stars themselves. He filled a portion of that vast emptiness with himself. His entire body shook with the sweet, savage joy of coming alive.

See Rajiv Moté's story "L'Appel du Vide" online at Metaphorosis.
If you liked it, leave a comment. Authors love that!
Remember to subscribe to our e-mail updates so you'll know when new stories are posted.

About the story

"L'Appel du Vide," French for "the call of the void," is a phenomenon where a person standing at a precipice has the unreasonable, outrageous urge to step out into the abyss. Psychologists have studied this, and found that the urge isn't suicidal, but an act of imagination that sparks the awareness of being alive. I wrote this story for a class on Magic As Metaphor in fiction, which I took during a year of unemployment, after quitting my job with no 'next move' in hand. It wasn't lost on me how much privilege it required just to walk away. It was a scary, frustrating, guilt-ridden year of feeling like I had made a terrible mistake, wondering if I was too old to make a career change or even re-enter my career, and realizing I'd become a burden on my family. It was also the most wonderful, freeing period of my adult life. Where once I lived in the interstices, I suddenly controlled big blocks of time on my calendar. I could use them to pursue things that engaged my intellect and interests. I could spend more time with people I cared about. I was never bored. It wouldn't—couldn't—last, but having a taste of that life was transformative in ways I'm still discovering. This is a story about having that taste. Of knowing you have to go back, but still relishing that moment on the brink of a larger world.

A question for the author

Q: What five words describe you?

A: Paying attention while simultaneously daydreaming.

About the author

Rajiv Moté is a writer and software engineering manager living in Chicago with his wife, daughter, and puppy. He'd pick the superpower of flight over invisibility any day, and the dreams in which he's flying are the best he's ever had. He'll relax at parties only if engaged about wine, comic books, epic fantasy, 80s music, NPR podcasts, or by a friendly dog.

www.rajivmote.com, @RajivMote

The Color of My Home is Red Like an Apple

Evan Marcroft

The color of my home is red like an apple. That is what God told the father of all my fathers, who told all their daughters, who told me. I do not know what an apple is, only that it is sweet and red like my home. My name is Anan. I have lived as long as nine suns, and I have always served God.

When I was a baby, my father was chosen to be Nurse of God. As expected, he involved me in all the procedures of pleasing God. Every day, my clutchmates and I were brought before Him to play in the sand, for God delights in the happiness of children. When we grew older we were allowed outside the village to spearfish along the river where our mwku'oh cattle drink. The fat of scuttlefish, when rendered, made good oil with which to polish God's body, and their shells were fitting gifts for children to give.

I have seen nine suns live and die now, and it has since become my duty to help clean God. This morning, as every morning, we five chosen gather outside my family's house and walk together behind my father to the great tent where God lives. My father says that when He came to live with us my people had no village, but wandered after the mwku'oh with our homes rolled up upon our sledges.

Today the daggerwind rages, blasting the village with the desert's glass dust, and so the panels of His house are tied shut. We enter only with my father's permission, bent low in respect.

Inside we find that God has written a greeting in the sand for us. *Hello to you, my children,* he says. *I hope that all of you are well this day.* We knuckle dutifully and begin our work. Nananqi and her sister Wocamhsh scrub clean the wrinkles of His old feet, while Tsuvuyé shines His one huge eye. Yonweh, with her small hands, brushes out the crevices of his body. I alone have the prized task of polishing the golden wings through which God drinks the light. My friends smolder with envy, but I am the daughter of the Nurse, and so it is my right. God never said I could not be proud.

Sweeping my fingers across the glittering planes of God's wings, I can feel the captured fire crackling within. Not even from His own welcome do I feel more blessed than in these moments. His body is stronger than bone and stone. Through drought and famine, storm and stagnation, God will be with us. With me.

When we are finished God scrawls His thanks with His one protracting arm. The characters for *gratitude, smile, to you,* toned by a precise inclination of His eye. *Know, children, that I appreciate you all,* God says, and my hearts bake in his warmth. There was a time when He first came to live with us when none of this was understood. But in His patience He taught my people to make sounds with shapes and so learn to commune with Him. Everything we Hhmuadi have, we owe to him. It was he who taught us to sculpt river mud into houses that could withstand the daggerwind's wroth, and to fashion that wild glass into windows. It was He who tutored us in the natural hierarchy of men and women so that we would no longer live in our incorrect way.

As always, we pray to Him before we go, knuckles to our hearts, for the strength of our crops and for the fullness of the river, for a path to the Blue Star after death.

Sometimes God replies. This time He does not.

Outside God's home, the village is bustling. The daggerwind has calmed, and the earth glitters like clear water. Families are rolling up the thick glass-catching cloaks on their houses to let in the light. The wives are heading to the field to reap needlecane. I spy a group of young men entering from the eastern gate with a dead wraraqwa on a sledge behind them. The ferocious cactus-beast is a full twenty hands long, and still bloated with the blood of its last meal. It will make a fine addition to tomorrow's feast.

All Hmuadi have their work to do before then, and I am no exception. Women's chores keep me busy throughout the day. There are mwku'oh to bleed for nectar, water to pull from the river and boil. When the sun begins to settle into the claws of the Mimirtaigh Mountains, I go with the women to ready tomorrow's feast, stripping the sweet fruit from venomous needlecane by mazarine twilight and then by firelight. No matter how hard I am worked I do not complain— not now, not ever before. I accept the role that God has given me, both its blessings and its burdens. Neither do I cheat or steal, or strike others in anger. I should not fear to be chosen come tomorrow.

Nevertheless, when I at last crawl into my rootthread bedding, my stomach churns as though worm-ridden. So much rides upon such a small span of time. Tomorrow, those of us children who have lived as long as nine suns will gather before God to receive his blessing—to be chosen. After that, I will be a woman in full, ready to marry and make sons and daughters of my own. And when I die God will send me to the Blue Star, to live with my ancestors along the florid banks of a river free of illness and pain.

I should not worry. I know I am virtuous. But still, sleep comes slowly.

There is a long day between now and then.

My hearts beat along to the frantic rhythm of the Choosing Song. I have witnessed this rite many times from the amongst the crowd, and though I dreamed of the day I myself would stand here at the door God's house, at the cusp of womanhood, somehow I never understood the reality of it, the soon-ness of it.

There are thirteen of us who will now be as old as ten suns. We kneel on the raked dirt outside God's house in stoic silence, in contrast to the revelry around us. I watch the young men regale spellbound children with the tale of yesterday's hunt, pantomiming the wraraqwa's snarling death. My own brother Mangiirse, the tallest and strongest, leads his friends in a drunken hunting hymn.

I remember how proudly he went to God at his Becoming two suns past, already a brave hunter. I have nothing to be proud of but my obedience. I wonder if I will be able hold my head as high. I wonder, quietly, if my obedience will be enough.

Finally, but long after my legs have gone numb, my father emerges from the crowd and raises his hands, hushing the village. Behind him, I can see men hoisting the windows of God's house. The silence deepens as his holy body comes into view. In this place he has resided since he arrived from across the Sea of Stars. How great a God he is, to surrender heaven and live contentedly among us like an old grandfather.

My father beckons to the boy closest him. All the boys will go before the girls, no matter that I am the daughter of God's Nurse. So it has always been. My father leads the boy into God's house. It is hard to see, but I know what happens. A happy murmur ripples through the crowd.

I realize soon that my faster wishes to save me for last. The other eleven children go by in what seems like seconds. All are chosen, all are flung into the embrace of the crowd to be met as new men and women, beloved strangers. Finally my father reaches for me, and I come unsteadily to his waiting hand.

I have been in the presence of God more times than I can count, yet kneeling before Him now, it feels as though I am beholding Him for the first time. I know rationally that he is not much taller than me, but from down here He seems a monolith. His body gleams like a geode, His surfaces smooth as ice and indestructible as the world itself. His fathomless eye swivels and fixates upon me. What does God think about, I wonder. What could trouble a mind as great as His?

His arm pivots towards me, the joints of His complex hand whirring softly. It hangs over me like a fate. My breath catches in my chest. I hover at the invisible seam between past and future, where one person ends and another begins.

I clench my eyes shut. I wait for His touch.

And it does not come.

In my head I stretch the moment as long as I can, giving it chance after chance, until I am forced to open my eyes. The hand of God trembles above me as if gripped by something unseen. The lens of his eye dilates and contracts at random. I do not so much hear the horror spreading through the crowd as feel it, a blistering chill upon my back.

My people are realizing slowly that my future has come, and I am not one of them.

My father's hand closes around my shoulder, and a sudden, saw-toothed wail tears its way out of my throat. I rear up, thrashing away from him. He recoils as one would from a snapping beast. Fear uglies his face. Fear of *me*. The red earth beneath me teeters like a plate balanced on a stone. I run for my home, and the gathered village parts for me as though I am diseased.

I am to be exiled.

The deliberations were short. I am not the first to be refused by God, and nothing should be different because I am the daughter of his Nurse. I am no longer Hhmuadi, and so the obligations of kinship are not owed to me. No man will condescend to marry me, and even if I am raped, any children I might bear would be tsöach matat—refused from birth. As a girl-woman with no use, I and my possible offspring would pose a drain on the village's resources. But more than that, I am abhorrent in the eye of God. My former people will not suffer me to pain him with my presence.

Of course I must go. I can respect the logic.

But still, it hurts. Like a death that does not end.

At sunrise the morning after my refusal, my father rouses me from my bed of blankets and leads me to the edge of the village. My father provides me with a heavy cloak, a bundle of provisions, a horn of water, and a lavaglass knife. There is sadness in my father's eyes, but resolution in his jaw. I am to walk in a straight line to the East, into the desert, and never return.

I do not get far before the thought of my family breaks me and I come running back. If I can just see their faces one last time, take them fresh into the desert with me, then everything will be alright. I promise that I won't mind dying. I know that he will understand. He is still my father.

I do not take six steps before a stone from his sling catches me in the leg, and I crumble into the sand.

This time he and another man gag me and carry me far out into the desert. This time, when he lets me go, I see in his expression that the next stone will find my eye. The last I will ever see of my father is his determination to kill me.

The time, I walk as I am told until when I look back all I see behind me is a plane of red sand and powdered glass cut into two infinite halves by my hoofprints. Within hours, that umbilicus will be blown away by the wind, and nothing will connect be to my home but the aching hollow in me molded to its shape. I fall to my knees where I am and wait for the desert to take me. I do not cry; I am somewhere far past that.

The fickle desert does not take me, and so I continue toward that uncertain place where it will. An empty day passes before I find shelter beneath an overlapping of stone slabs, and stagger into the hollow beneath to faint. Swaddled in my cloak, I somehow I survive the hateful cold of the night, and in the morning I plan the direction I will go to die.

The desert continues uninterrupted into the east further than my knowledge of the land extends. Far to the south is the Sharp Ocean, a whorl of glass knives taller than ten men standing end on end, whose reaches have yet to be explored by my people. There is no life there, no water, no respite from the sun. Surely it would kill me. But to the north are the Mimirtaigh Mountains, forbidden to my people by God since a day long forgotten. It is said that to be caught in their shadow is to be hidden from God's love. Thinking on it, I find the old taboos no longer feel so dire. And I am forsaken already.

I walk for what seems like the lifespan of a hundred suns. I had never understood how vast the desert was. When you are young, the world is only as big across as the furthest thing away you know of. But the world does not care what you know. My rations and water do not last long. I starve and thirst until I stumble upon a dried-up oasis and lap up the last of its muddy water. I find a few small, hardy fruits in the sand and stay the night. The next day I am forced to scurry up a heap of rock to escape a stampede of wild mwku'oh, lest I be chewed to slurry under their threshing cilia. Another day, I am given only minutes to burrow under the ground by the howl of a nearby Thirsting Tree. I try not to choke on sand and powdered glass as the towering monster lumbers over my hiding place, snuffling after the scent of moisture.

But in between these frenetic moments is nothing. Burning nothing. Freezing nothing. I almost welcome the danger when it comes.

I try, and fail, to not think of my family.

Sand eventually gives way to dirt. Little by little, the mountains rise up beneath me like pregnant bellies. As night falls and their shadow inches over me, I feel no more cursed than before. I do not know what kinds of beasts make the mountains their home, so I do not know what to fear. The trek is no easier or more difficult than it was through the desert, only steeper. I suck sour water from pools I find in bowls of rock. I gnaw roots and look for more when they don't kill me. I sleep in the cracks between great stony teeth, and wonder when the world will think to scrape me loose.

It does not take long. On my third evening in the mountains, dark clouds begin to dew on the glass of the sky. I am quick to abandon hours of forward progress to scuttle back to a cave I know is safe; I reach shelter moments before the storm hits like a hammer. It is the wind's wailing that nearly kills me; it masks the howl of something else.

I do not hear the Thirsting Tree until it is upon me.

I have no time to react, and nowhere to run, as the narrow cave mouth is invaded by a thicket of grasping tentacles. My leg is enveloped immediately and numbed by the monster's venom. I am ripped from the mountainside like a dagger from a sheath. Frigid rain pelts me as a dangle over the monster's canopy. Its clawed roots grip the rock above my hiding place, a spearfisher perched to harpoon. I watch a flower-shaped mouth bloom amidst its writhing boughs—the face of so many Hhmuadi nightmares—and unspool dozens of spear-tipped tongues.

I do cry then, because I am only ten suns old and never became a woman.

But I also grope for the knife at my hip and, curling towards my feet, slash it through the Tree's boneless hand. Its scream defeats all other sounds; the pressure on my leg disappears. I squeeze my eyes shut, expecting a painful fall. Instead there is a light that pierces my eyelids, and a sound like a beaten drum as wide as a village. Something hits me hard in the side, and the next I know I am tumbling end over end down a muddy slope. I glimpse the Thirsting Tree teetering far above me, blazing like a torch. Then my head strikes a protruding stone, and I cease to think.

Some time later I awake. It is still storming, and I am still hurting. I lie in mud, at the bottom of a gorge. Beside me is the body of the Thirsting Tree, split down the middle and smoldering noisomely. In that struggling light I make out another figure. A single, crooked arm. A flat black eye. Outflung wings, in which flecks of gold glisten.

God watches me die.

I stir at something clanking. I sit up out my bed of mud and look around for the sound. The awareness that I am alive flitters unobtrusively through my head. The sun is out again, and I can see clearly that God is there, no further than thirty hoofspans away. He is drumming statically on His back for no reason that I can see other than to get my attention.

For a moment I swoon with rage. God, who has never moved from His house in generations, has come all this way to mock me in my suffering. But there is something about Him that chills me almost simultaneously.

The God I knew was pristine white and silver. This God is utterly caked in earth, and where His body is exposed, I see now that it is a dull red like the earth of this world. I creep cautiously closer. My God's feet were lovingly cared-for; the plates of this God's feet have come unraveled and sunk into the ground, as if He has stood here for a hundred suns. And on my God's chest, where He had worn a square of red, white, and blue stripes, He now wears one that is all red with a speckling of gold stars.

This is not my God, I realize. This is a different God altogether.

He stops tapping on himself as I approach Him as I would a wounded animal, staying well out of reach of His hand. I do not trust this God to be as gentle as my own. His eye swivels haltingly to fix on me; I can see that He is nearly blind with clinging filth. Over the course of a minute, He laboriously scratches something into the hard mud in front of Him; intrusive plants infest the joints of His arm. I squint to read His message. *Do not be afraid.* The same first words my God ever wrote that my people understood.

"Are you... God?" I ask. I have to be sure.

He writes the negative symbol. *No.*

Before I can reply, He begins to scrape out something else. *You Hhmuadi,* He says, after much effort. *You come from place where God is, yes? Us hope to see you for long time.* This not-God speaks his own language poorly. His grammar is full of holes. He uses the symbol for 'us' when He should say 'me.' *If you come see me later than now, this tool may die waiting.*

"Why did you never move from this spot?" I ask.

This tool broken on landing. I can see Him struggling to articulate himself. His diction is the simplest possible. *Am immobile.*

"Where did you come from?" I must wait for Him to brush away old words before He can draw new ones.

We provide this tool from place called Blue Star.

I frown. "You look like God, and you come from the Blue Star," I say, "But you say you are not God, and you call yourself a tool. I am sorry—I do not understand."

The symbols for me, name, question. *What is your name?*

"Anan," I answer, uneasily.

Hello Anan. You are able to call us Morning Star. We are sorry, but your God lied to you.

I sit cross-legged before Morning Star, no longer fearful of him, because he is too old and broken to hurt me. He has listened to my story, and I now I will listen to his.

His writing is less ponderous now that I have washed the sand from his joints and pulled out most of the weeds. *To begin,* he says, *the Blue Star is not a paradise. Hhmuadi do not go there when they die. It is a world like this one, but very far away. You could live one thousand times and never walk there. It is not a place of joy and plenty. There is as much death as there is here. There is even more death than there is here, for there are many more people.*

"But you said there are no Hhmuadi there."

Another kind of people live there. They look very different from you. You would think them monsters if you saw them.

"How many are there?" I ask, challengingly.

I wait as Morning Star inscribes a number, and then adds degrees of multiplication to that number, until he exceeds the limits of what is possible. I scoff at the absurdity of it, a number so large it has no name. The Blue Star must be carpeted in people as thickly as the desert is carpeted in grains of sand.

I tell only the truth, Anan, Morning Star chides. *And it was they who sent me here a long time ago, as they sent your God here even longer before that. You must understand that your God and I are not living things as you are. We are a kind of tool. We are masks-that-walk, mindless as dirt. The people of the Blue Star could not come here themselves, so they sent these tools to see through. To live through.*

"That does not make any sense," I sneer. "No-one can make a tool that walks and speaks like a person. How can a tool love the way God does?"

The people of the Blue Star are very clever, Anan. We know many secrets of the universe that you Hhmuadi do not. We make sledges that float in the sky. We have weapons that can knock down mountains. You cannot even dream of what is possible for us.

"Us?" I ask, and in the very next moment, I coldly understand. I think of the loretellers of my village who through magic-seeming trickery can throw their voice wherever they like, sometimes even into another's mouth. I think of the yeyemocawh, the Laughing Hole, that mouthsome predator who sings the songs of other animals to lure prey into its warren.

Yes, says Morning Star, observing the change in my expression. *You are speaking with us right now, through this tool. There are many of us present, instructing the tool what to say. Just as there are many others telling your God what to say.*

"That's not true," I snap without meaning to. My face is growing hot. My hearts begin rail like captives against the cage of my chest. "You're lying."

If that thing is God, then what am I? Morning Star makes a sympathetic gesture with his eye. *We understand your doubts. You fear what it would mean if it were true. You fear that it was not divine will that ruled your life, but instead the whim of mere people hidden behind a curtain. You fear that you worshipped something no greater than yourself. You fear that you were cast out from your family for no good reason. But you told us you have always been virtuous, and we trust you. So why would God reject you unless it did not matter to him?*

"Why?" I demand, shooting to my feet. "If that is all true, what would they deceive my people for, and why for so long?" I am too heated to catch myself saying *them* instead of *Him*.

It was not their intention. They sent their mask here to study your world, to know the Hhmuadi. But your people met saw their mask and called it God. They of the Blue Star decided it would be easier to let them believe that. You might not have cooperated otherwise.

My life, and the lives of my family, those of my ancestors, whose hearts all cleaved so dearly to God's wisdom—all just pretend games. All of us, led along from birth to death by nothing more than a hand puppet. Of course I fear that be to be true. I flinch from the notion as I would from something venomous. But for all my want, I do not know the words to argue.

Even now I am compelled to defend God against these evil words. He was as much as father to me as the man who sired me. It was God who raised my soul, if not my body. But I try and try and still cannot see the logic in damning me to die in the desert when all I have for Him is love. My tongue is prone beneath a thousand excuses, each as light and thin as shed skin.

They say that God knows what lies down paths unseen. But I do not have his eyes.

Morning Star steps into the silence I leave him. *We of the Blue Star are not one tribe like you are. We are two, and we have fought for a very long time. At first, there were too many of us for our world to provide for everyone so we had to fight for food and water and land. Now there is little left to fight for, and we fight because we hate each other. It was the enemy tribe who sent the mask you call God to your world. They wanted to know if it were possible to travel there and take your food and water and land. They wanted to condition you for their arrival in the future. We could not let them be the only ones on your world, and so we sent our own mask —this mask. When they make one spear, we make two. When they make ten arrows, we make one hundred. That is the way of our world.*

"You must want the same thing, then," I say, miserably. "You want to take our world to feed your own. If your mask had not broken, we would worship you instead."

Most likely. Your world hangs like an apple among the stars.

I snort a surprised and unhappy laugh. "You should lie about something like that."

Why would we? We have stopped our enemies from setting out for your world many times. Not for your sake, but simply to spite them. They have done the same to us. Many believe we may already be out of time. That the apple is out of reach. So we have no reason to lie to you.

"Then what were you waiting for all this time?"

We have told you the truth you would never have learned otherwise. Now we ask that you do something for us. He scribbles something more. The symbols for 'return,' 'home,' 'destroy—'

Go back to your village and destroy God.

The first word to find its way back to my stunned lips is, "Why?"

This tool will soon break. We do not want our enemy to be the only presence on your world. If not us, then no-one. That is all.

"No," I say, "No, no, I can't do that."

What do you owe it?

My family, my home, everything I love, one half of me declares. The other half whispers, *everything that was taken.* "I can't just believe you," I say pleadingly. "You tell me that all I know is a lie. How can I know that is not a lie as well? You are no better than God, to tell me what is real with no proof." If there is a real world then let me stand upon it, I silently demand, or I will forget you for a fever dream and continue on to where I die.

Morning Star raises his hand to bid me be quiet. *A fair complaint, Anan. There is a rock behind you. Go and bring it to us. With it, we will prove the truth of all we have told you.*

I glance back at the dun-red stone he speaks of and go to pry it from the ground. It is no easy task, for I am withered from my slog through the desert. A thousand crawling things skitter out from underneath it as I roll it into my hands. The earth-chilled mass of it threatens to pull me over as I lug it back to Morning Star. Swung by a larger man, its sharp spine would cave through a head like a fist through an egg.

I return to find Morning Star with his neck bent, his eye downturned. His arm is tautly horizontal. He has left one final message for me scrimshawed into the ground.

This tool cannot move properly. It will soon cease to function entirely. It has no further use to us but this. Let it become the proof that you require.

The stone you hold is the fruit of knowledge.

Swing it hard.

I stare at the words for an endless time. And then I raise the rock above my head.

At night, my village is as silent as any other patch of the desert. I creep beneath windowsills, silent as an illness, walking on my hands when necessary. I have padded my hooves with a poultice of resin and grass to mute my footsteps.

I do not linger near my family's house unnecessarily, though I long with both hearts to peer inside and see how my family has changed in the time I have been gone. To see if my baby sister has grown her teeth, if Mangiirse has earned the starglass hero-knife he always coveted. Perhaps they have not changed at all. They have not been through the desert as I have.

Never more clearly have I beheld God's influence on my village, the invisible scaffolding of His tutelage standing around my house, articulating its dimensions, constraining its possibilities. Our laws are given, our roles assigned, our language taught. I cannot imagine what we might have become if God had never come.

A teacher is both the giver and keeper of knowledge. For every good thing he gave us, there must be a thousand things he withheld. A thousand paths along which my people might have walked. Without him we might wander the desert still, desperately chasing food and water. But with him we cannot help but camp in his light.

With him, we wander nowhere.

Only one man keeps watch outside the House of God. It is his solemn duty to sleep in the day and guard God at night. Rather than face his brawn and lavaglass club, I wait until his patrol around the House takes him out of sight, and then slip inside from the rear.

God's form slowly resolves from the darkness like an animal imperfectly camouflaged. I hold my breath and wait for any sign that He is awake. I wave my hand before His eye to see if He will stir.

"Can you hear me?" I whisper, as loudly as I dare. "Please, God. Tell me you are real," I can't help but ask of him. "I need you."

And even now, it is true.

Even now, I crave His absolute world. How could I not? All the happiness I ever knew was in the fist of a greater power. We Hhmuadi are not the product of our own will, and even now I could die with that, so long as I could believe it meant something.

"Tell me that you're real." I beg to be saved from the unknowable wilds of a godless future, for my world to be clutched like a sweet, red apple, so long as it is held with love. "Tell me I am wrong. Just tell me. Please."

I wait, but I receive no answer, and I know that it is not refusal. Whether He is God or the mask of one, he is simply not there.

Perhaps it is night on the Blue Star.

I undo the sling I wear across my shoulder and cup in my hands the jag of rock that I painstakingly carried here from the mountains, across a gulf of sand and time.

I must be efficient, for the guard is close by. There is no hesitance in me; my faith has never been stronger than in this moment. I am without doubt that the great truth of God could never be shattered by just a girl with a stone.

See Evan Marcroft's story "The Color of My Home is Red Like an Apple" online at Metaphorosis.
If you liked it, leave a comment. Authors love that!
Remember to subscribe to our e-mail updates so you'll know when new stories are posted.

About the story

This story emerged from a lifelong grappling with the fundamental hurdle that I perceived in the concept of religion. I was never one to put faith in any process that could not be studied directly, and so I was somewhat puzzled by those in my life who held up the laws of their faith as objective, somehow inherent to the universe, although I could respect the joy their beliefs brought into their lives. From my subjective point of view, these individuals were being pushed to become or do things for the sake of precepts laid down long before they were born, that they were in fact born into, without a choice. This story is an expression of my philosophy, which is not that religion is automatically untrue, but rather that faith — as well as its associated codes — should be a choice, that nothing deserves to be done just because it's what was done before you. The Hhmuadi in this story may be happy with the lives that their god has given them, but at the same time they were denied the chance to have any other sort of life of their own creation. They are willing and yet unwilling bearers of its will. When Anan destroys that god at the end of the story, she is not overthrowing some tyrannical rule, but rather giving her people the choice to either move on from the culture that her god has created or remain in it in the faith that their god, even broken, is true. Either outcome is good so long as it is what they want.

A question for the author

Q: If you could have any super power, what would it be?

A: If I could have any one super power, I would want the ability to experience alternate realities at will.

While I do love being a writer, I often find myself wondering at all the opportunities I passed up to pursue that life. The world is full of more people than I will ever be able to meet. There are too many things for me to possibly do in just a hundred or so years. I wouldn't necessarily want the power to fulfill any dream I might have, but rather the ability to pursue any dream I cared to, with all the ups and downs that chase would entail. The best part of any journey is going there, after all. Plus, I might uncover an alternate reality where I have other superpowers too, so really there's no downside to this.

About the author

Evan Marcroft is a half-blind yeti-person with a sideways foot and an allergy to the sun. When he was a child he dreamed of writing important works of Earth-shaking beauty and settled for writing fantasy and science fiction instead. He currently lives in Sacramento California with a cat and a loving wife who foolishly believes he'll someday make real money doing this. You can find his other works at *Pseudopod*, *Strange Horizons*, and *Mirror Dance*, as well as here at *Metaphorosis*. You can reach him on Twitter at @Evan_Marcroft and contact him for any reason at Evanmarcroft@hotmail.com.

Copyright

Metaphorosis Publishing

Metaphorosis offers beautifully written science fiction and fantasy. Our projects include:

Metaphorosis Magazine

Metaphorosis, a weekly magazine of SFF short stories, including stories from all the authors in this anthology. Find out more at magazine.metaphorosis.com, and sign up to be notified of new stories.

Metaphorosis Books

Recent books from Metaphorosis can be found at **books.metaphorosis.com**, and include:

Metaphorosis 2017

Metaphorosis 2016

All the stories from *Metaphorosis* magazine's second year.

Almost all the stories from *Metaphorosis* magazine's first year.

Metaphorosis: Best of 2017

The best science fiction and fantasy stories from *Metaphorosis'* 2nd year.

Metaphorosis: Best of 2016

The best science fiction and fantasy stories from *Metaphorosis'* 1st year.

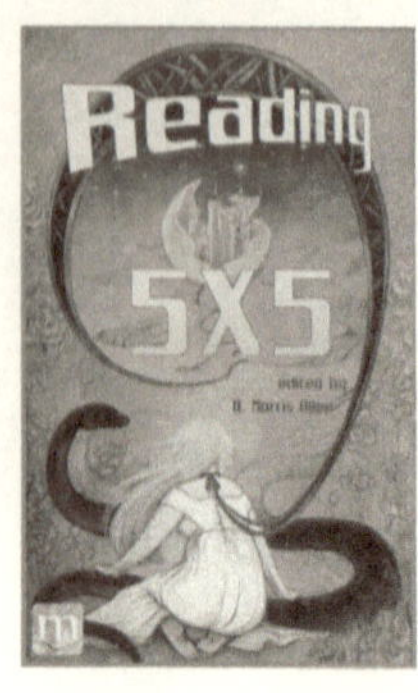 

Reading 5X5

Five stories, five times

Twenty-five SFF authors, five base stories, five versions of each – see how different writers take on the same material.

Reading 5X5

Writers' Edition

All the stories from the regular, readers' edition, plus two extra stories, the story seed, and authors' notes.

Best Vegan SFF of 2017

Best Vegan SFF of 2016

The best vegan science fiction and fantasy stories of 2017!

The best vegan science fiction and fantasy stories of 2016!

Susurrus

A darkly romantic story of magic, love, and suffering.